EVERYTHING SHE THOUGHT

CIN MEDLEY

MED'S PUB

EVERYTHING *She* THOUGHT

CIN MEDLEY

For my beautiful Britt, you are forever my heart.
I love you, beautiful girl.

Published by: Med's Pub Publishing
Copyright © 2020 Cin Medley
All Rights Reserved
ISBN-13: 978-0-9989748-8-0
Cover Design by Amanda Walker
P.A. and Design Services
Edited by Kendra Gaither at Kendra's
Editing and Book Services
Formatting by Med's Pub Publishing

CHAPTER ONE

KARL

Karl walked into the restaurant after yet another long night. He smiled at the hostess, and she smiled back.

"Mr. Anders, table for one?"

"Yes, it's just me this morning."

After grabbing a menu, she stepped around her podium, brushing against him. "Follow me. Would you like a window seat or a booth?"

As he followed her cute, tight ass across the room, he leaned in and spoke softly. "Window, please."

The young girl giggled. He knew she wanted him. She always flirted with him when he came here. But today, Karl felt a bit disgusted with himself. This was the third woman in the past ten days that he'd slept with. He couldn't remember why he was doing this anymore. The money was great; shit was it ever. It afforded him a great apartment on the beach and his own gym. But was it worth it? He was going on forty-eight, lying about his age to stay in the game. These women and his boss thought he was just thirty-nine. But this was his great opportunity to live the American dream. To be and to have all the things he had never had.

As they moved through the restaurant, his eyes always scanned to make sure he didn't see someone he knew, some other client. It was a habit, especially after the huge confrontation he had a few months back. Walking into a restaurant the morning after, with the date from the night before, only to run into a date he'd had the week before. It wasn't a good idea to have such things take place. For this, he was grateful no one knew his real name. Jon Anders was the name he used in his professional life. Karl Hagger was the name his mother gave him at birth.

The lovely young woman placed his menu on a table, that looked out over the water. "Here you go, sir. Rebecca will be your server."

"Thank you." Sitting down, he looked out on the water, wondering what the fuck he was doing. His mother wouldn't approve of the life he was living. In his defense, he started shortly after coming to America, when he'd needed the money. Looking back on all those years ago, after coming off his service to the Army, he wanted the American dream. He wanted the American women, with their wild eyes and hard bodies. He could remember listening to his buddies talking about American women, how easy they were, how hungry for sex they were. He couldn't imagine that being true. He was a gentleman, having been raised by a woman who taught him to value the things a woman had to offer.

Shaking his head, he chuckled to himself. These women here, well, they were wild, especially after a few drinks. He knew he wasn't a bad-looking man. He'd started shaving his head when the grey hair became too noticeable. He was, after all, telling people he was younger than he was. His hand moved to his face, brushing his trimmed beard. As each day passed, more and more grey hair showed up. Prematurely grey he would tell these women. He was a man with an insatiable sexual appetite. He loved women, he loved the female body, and he knew how to make it a gratifying experience for them. Not that it wasn't gratifying for him, but none of them ever cared to take their time with him. He had discovered that they were all greedy for what he could give them, do to them.

A woman cleared her throat, and he turned his head to see who it was.

"Hi, I'm Rebecca. Can I get you some coffee?"

Karl smiled at her and nodded. "That would be great. Thank you."

"Do you know what you would like?"

"Just two eggs, over easy, with toast and some orange juice, please."

He watched as she wrote down his order, then she poured him a cup of coffee and walked away. His eyes now scanned the room to see if his date would appear, as they did from time to time, just to get a few more minutes with him. But he was off the clock, and his life was waiting for him back in Miami. As he was turning back to the water, his eyes caught on a woman sitting across the room, her brow furrowed as she looked down at the tablet in her hand. Her glasses were perched across the bridge of her nose, and her hair, dark auburn, with streaks of grey running through it, was bunched up on top of her head in a messy bun. He couldn't really see what kind of body she had, but her face, as far as he could tell, was bare of makeup. Her hair shined under the lights of the restaurant, looking clean and natural. He was finding it foreign to see a woman in such a natural way. All the women he encountered had far too much makeup on, and their hair, well, he always knew that when he touched it, he would be met with the resistance of hairspray.

A waiter approached her, and when she looked up and smiled at him, Karl heard himself moan. *Fuck!* She was stunning. Not his usual choice. Her face had a few years on it, but she wore those years well. He saw her nodding, and when the waiter walked away, her eyes moved back to her tablet. Karl knew he was staring at her, so he turned his head. His waitress came back with his food, a reason to turn his head back in her direction. But as he ate, he kept shifting his gaze back to the beautiful woman. Her waiter brought her a pot of hot water, and she thanked him, then he watched as she pulled a tea bag from her bag on the chair next to her. He was mesmerized as she bobbed the bag up and down in the cup without looking at it, keeping her eyes glued to whatever it was she was reading.

Long after his plate was taken away, he sat there, just casually watching her. His heart jumped when she slipped her tablet into the leather bag next to her as she stood to leave. She wore a light pink blouse with a long grey skirt and what looked like black biker boots.

After taking money out of her purse and dropping it on the table, she lifted her head and her eyes landed on his, causing his breath to hitch in his chest. She stood there for what seemed to him was minutes, but it was really only a few seconds. He nodded in her direction and smiled a small smile. She nodded back at him and then turned to walk away. The minute his eyes landed on her ass, he knew there was more to her than the women he was used to. This woman he gawked at was the type of woman he never imagined he would be interested in. He was used to women with hard bodies, nice firm asses, and perky tits. They were his version of the American dream. They were everything his buddies talked about, everything he believed he wanted. His eyes followed her as she moved through the restaurant toward the door. Standing, he casually followed her out, finding her standing at the front desk of the hotel when he reached the door. His head jerked in the direction of the front doors when he heard a woman yell out.

"Mel!"

He turned back as she spun her body around, the smile that crossed her face stunning him. She was breathtaking, moving toward the woman who had called her name. Karl stood leaning against the wall, watching the two women. Then a third walked in.

"Oh my God, Mel. You came."

The three women hugged and moved toward the stairs. He couldn't hear what they were saying, but he felt compelled to follow them. By the time he reached the second floor, they had disappeared. On this floor of the hotel were conference rooms, each with a sign at the doorway. He walked down the hall, looking at and reading the signs. In the middle of the hall, he stopped as he read the sign. *Writing Expose with guest speaker Mel Cross.* He knew her name was Mel, so was this her? Quietly, he opened the door and moved into the room, taking a seat at the back. As he looked around, he noticed that the room was filled mostly with women. There were a few men, so he felt comfortable enough to stay. The lights dimmed, and a woman walked up to a podium.

"Ladies and gentlemen, I want to welcome you to our writer's expose. Here today, in our workshops, we have some of the best writers available to answer your questions and help you in any way they can. Then tomorrow, I hope you'll join us for our tenth annual author event, where you can meet all our participating authors to have your books signed. This year, we are lucky to have fifteen models joining us for pictures, as well. It is sure to be a huge success, and for those of you who have purchased tickets, we have our annual Masquerade ball." The crowd applauded.

Karl sat in the back, now intrigued. He saw a pamphlet sitting on the chair next to him and picked it up, looking through it. Her picture was in it with a brief statement.

Mel Cross, guest speaker: Mel has been writing for 15 years, with 8 best sellers. Her new release, Everything She Thought, soared to the New York Times best-seller list within 3 days.

Mel will deliver the opening speech, with her topic, 'Inspiration in writing. What makes us write?'

Lifting his head to look toward the podium, the woman continued. "Let's give the warmest of welcomes to Mel Cross." The place erupted in applause, and everyone stood as she walked up to the microphone. Once everyone was sitting, she stood there smiling.

"Hello, everyone. I'm glad to be here; although, I'm not so sure why I was chosen. Standing here looking out at you all, I see some familiar faces, some known faces, and a great many new faces. I am sure that there are many of you out there who are far more qualified to be giving this talk than I am."

Karl was shocked at the sound of her voice. He needed to be closer to her, so he tried to move unobtrusively from row to row, getting closer to the podium as she spoke.

"As many of you know," she smiled at the two women who had approached her in the lobby of the hotel, "I've been out of the circle for a long time now. Sometimes, I suppose, life grabs us all and holds us down. I'm sure everyone in this room knows what I am talking about." Karl noticed her eyes weren't as bright as they had been in the lobby. "But that's not what we are here to talk about now, are we? No, it's not. We are here to talk about inspiration, which I'm not sure we can really pinpoint any particular inspiration. I believe it's different for each of us. For me, well, it's several things. These flowers right here, or that door back there. The print on this lovely lady's blouse. The story comes from anywhere and everywhere. For me, when the inspiration comes, it's very hard to stop the story from unfolding. This new book, Everything She Thought, was a bit more real for me. The inspiration…" She paused. Karl watched as she wiped the tear off her cheek. "The inspiration came from here." She reached up and touched her heart.

He sat there, stunned like everyone else in the room. He watched her lick her lips several times, then slowly lift her head, looking at the woman who called out her name in the lobby. The woman stood and walked up to her, giving her a hug, and then watched as Mel walked away and left the room. He stood and followed her out the door as the other woman started talking. She was moving down the hall, disappearing behind a door he couldn't see but figured it was the restroom. So he just moved a bit closer and waited. When the doors to the conference room opened, the other woman in the lobby came out carrying the bag Mel had with her in the restaurant. She smiled at him as she walked by, disappearing into the same doorway.

He looked at the pamphlet in his hands and decided he looked a bit stalker-like, so he left, knowing he was going to a few, if not all, of the workshops. Making his way back to the front desk, he asked for a room and then procured himself tickets to the book signing and the masquerade ball the following night. There was something about this woman that made him think twice. He wanted to know what she was like. Smiling, he went to his car and grabbed his bag, then to the shop on the main level to buy a new suit and a mask.

CHAPTER TWO

MEL

"Mel, are you in here?" Kathy called out.

"Yeah, give me a minute." Blowing her nose, she opened the door and stepped into her friend's embrace. "I'm fine."

"No, you're not. I grabbed your bag." She handed her the bag.

"Thanks, I'm just going to head up to my room for a bit until the workshops start."

"Do you want to talk? Maybe get a drink?"

Mel laughed. "It's nine-thirty in the morning."

"It doesn't matter. If you need a drink, I'm your girl."

Mel hugged her. "No, I don't need a drink. I just need a few minutes to myself."

Kathy smiled at her. "All right, I'll see you later."

Mel left the bathroom and made it to her room, throwing her bag on the bed. "Fuck!" She was sure she would be able to handle the workshop. This was her life now, her paycheck. She had no choice in the matter. It took her nearly two years to be able to talk to another person. She just wanted the silence, time to have her own thoughts. She needed to remember that it was over. Falling onto the bed, she let out her breath and lay there on her back, staring at the ceiling. "Maybe I just need to get laid, have a wicked night of wild sex." She laughed out loud; how could she not? She had been responsible for her own orgasms for the last twenty-five years. Men did nothing but disappoint her, so getting randomly laid probably wasn't going to do anything for her. What she needed to do was get a grip. Her friends were downstairs covering for her. After washing her face in the bathroom, Mel looked in the mirror. "Get a fucking grip. It's time to move on. It's time for you now."

She stood there looking at her reflection, taking in the age lines now visible on her face, her eyes a shade of green she had never seen before. Sure, she'd earned every line, every wrinkle, every grey hair. Her life had been fantastic until three years ago. But it was done, and there was nothing she could do to change it. Pulling herself together, she grabbed her bag and pulled her phone out. Finding her playlist, she stuck her earbuds in her ears and hit play. Her mantra for the past year, 'What's Up?' by the 4 Non Blondes came blaring through the tiny speakers in her ears. She made her way to the elevator and headed back down to the workshops. When the doors opened, she was leaning against the back wall of the elevator with her eyes closed, her head bobbing up and down. Someone touched her arm. Her eyes shot open, and the bluest of blue eyes were smiling at her. Reaching up, she pulled one of the ear-buds out.

"Your floor?" he asked.

She looked out the door to see the second floor. "Sorry. Thank you." Pushing off the wall, she exited the elevator and moved down the hall, not looking back. The doors to the room where she was supposed to speak opened, and people flooded out. Her two friends, Kathy and Sue, found her. "Sue, thank you for covering for me. I'm so sorry for bailing. I have no idea what came over me. I guess I just wasn't ready for all this," Mel said.

"Don't even give it another thought. Shit happens. No biggie. So, what workshop are you going to first?"

"Well, I thought I would hang with you guys if that's all right."

"Oh, hell yeah, it is."

The three of them headed off, spending the day moving from one workshop to another. Seven hours later, they found themselves in the restaurant having dinner, laughing, and talking. For Mel, it was good to spend time with them. When this was over, she was headed to the beach for her birthday week, something she had done for years.

When they finished dinner, Mel excused herself. "Listen, I need to get some sleep, so you guys stay and have fun."

"Aren't you going to have a drink with us?" Kathy smiled at her.

"No, I don't drink anymore. I'm just going to order a bowl of fruit and head to my room. I'll see you bright and early. Tomorrow is going to be a long ass day, so maybe you shouldn't have too many drinks. There is the ball tomorrow night, too."

Sue's eyes got wide. "I think I'm with you, Mel. Come on, Kathy. We don't need to be hungover tomorrow."

"I suppose you're right. Let's just head to our room."

The three of them got up and headed to their rooms.

"I'll see you guys later. I need to get some stuff out of my car." Mel smiled at them. She just needed some fresh air and a few minutes to herself.

Karl

Karl sat at the same table he had that morning. He liked looking out at the water. He preferred the ocean view from his apartment, but any water view was the best view. He ordered a steak with a nice glass of red. He wasn't happy about running into his date from the night before. It's not what he wanted today. She was a lovely woman, beautiful, but she was shallow and hollow inside. There wasn't much to talk about; she was too busy, as were most of the women he dated, worrying about her looks.

As he sat there looking out at the water, he couldn't help but think about the past nine years he'd been there. He'd worked his ass of to become who he was. He owned his own gym, and this job afforded him the high rent. He had a great clientele, people he liked, people who trusted him. He was just having a hard time with the shallow end of this part-time job. He made some good friends; the guys were great. They'd often discussed why they became escorts, and with most men, they all agreed that they lived for the sex and the fact that there was no commitment involved. He was just a date for hire. What went on after the date was totally between two consenting adults. Not once did he feel anything more than basic attraction to any of the women.

Closing his eyes, he came to the realization that he was just as shallow as they were. He was tired of building them up, making them feel good for the time they spent together. He didn't sleep with all of them. Hell, he never made a move on any of them. They were always the aggressor. His buddies in the army were right about American women. But, then again, he was the asshole who never took the time to get to know any of them. It never felt real to him, and he was pretty sure it never felt real for them.

The waiter returned with his glass of wine. "Your meal will be ready in a few minutes. Is there anything I can get you while you wait?"

"No, thank you. I'm fine."

When the waiter walked away, Karl lifted his glass to his lips and saw her again. This time, she had on a pair of jeans and some sort of fancy top, and her hair was up in a ponytail. This morning, it had been in a messy bun on her head. When she turned as her friends walked in behind her, he saw how long it really was. "Jesus." The hostess walked them to the other side of the room. When she sat, her back was to him, which was probably a good thing because he didn't want to come off as some sort of stalker. *Isn't that what I am?* He chuckled to himself. *Get a fucking grip, Karl.* The waiter delivered his dinner, and he ate it but didn't really taste it. He needed to get out of the restaurant before he walked over there to talk to her.

When he finished, he paid the bill and headed out to take a walk and think. This wasn't who he was. It wasn't the type of man he had become, one who would go out of his way. Standing at the water's edge, his phone vibrated in his pocket. When he looked at it, his friend Tom's number was flashing.

"Hey."

"Hey, I thought you were coming back today. I was at the gym, and no one has seen you."

Turning, he looked at the hotel. "About that, I'm taking a few days off."

Tom laughed. "Don't tell me that chick got to you. What did I tell you? You can't fall for your dates."

Karl chuckled. "No, she wasn't much of a talker. I just feel like I need some time to myself."

"You need to talk?"

Karl didn't say anything for a long time. "Not yet. But maybe I do. We'll see."

"Listen, man, I'm here if you change your mind."

"Thanks, I'll see you when I get back."

He disconnected the call, considering maybe this wasn't the life he wanted anymore. He wanted to feel proud of himself and dating women for a price wasn't making him feel that way. If his mother knew what he was doing, she would be so disappointed in him. Hell, his father would disown him. But it was a secret he had hid for seven years now.

As he made his way back into the hotel, he saw her walking with a box in her arms and pulling what looked like a suitcase. The box wobbled in her arms, so he picked up his pace and made it to her just as it fell, reaching out to grab the box before it hit the ground.

"I got it."

She looked at him and smiled. "Oh, thank you so much."

He stood there looking at her. She didn't have an ounce of makeup on, and her skin glowed. He could see the fine lines of aging, light freckles along her cheek bones, and her eyes were a color of blue and green that he was sure he had never seen before. "Why don't you let me carry it for you?" He looked in the box.

Mel looked at him. "It's fine. I can do it." She reached for the box. "Would you be so kind and open the doors? That would be great."

"What kind of gentleman would I be if I opened the doors for a woman who was carrying everything, and I was carrying nothing?

Not a very good one." He reached for the box. "Let me do this to save face."

She laughed at him. "Fine, to save your reputation, you can carry the box."

"Thank you." He took the box and opened the door, letting her pass through it. His eyes traveled down to her ass. In her jeans, it looked magnificent—plump, not too thin, something to hold on to. *Jesus, get a fucking grip.*

The man at the front desk came rushing over. "Miss Cross, I'm sorry. I didn't see you struggling. Here, let me get this for you."

"It's fine. This lovely gentleman helped me. It's all right. Could you have a fruit salad sent to my room?"

"Of course, it will be there in fifteen minutes," he said.

"Thank you."

Karl just stood there looking at her. Everyone knew who she was. "So, Miss. I take it there isn't a Mr. waiting in the room to kick my ass when you open the door."

Smiling at him, she leaned in. "No mister and no door. Thank you for your help." She took the box from his hands. "I've got this. You have a lovely evening."

He didn't want her to leave, but damn if she didn't look good walking away from him. A smile was plastered across his face. The elevator doors opened, and she walked up to them like they were waiting for her. When she turned around, she smiled at him. "Goodnight."

He nodded. "Goodnight." And just like that, the doors closed, and she was gone.

Mel

When the elevator doors closed, Mel let out a breath she wasn't aware she'd been holding. "What the hell was that?" Her smile spread slowly across her lips. Those eyes were so blue, sparkling blue. "Where did he come from?"

The elevator stopped, and the doors opened. Shutting her door, she leaned against it. "Wow. Just wow." But her track record with men was not a good one. The mistake she made seventeen years ago drove it home that it wasn't a good idea to get involved with a man.

She knew who she was, and she knew she wanted to love and be loved by a man who was obsessed with her. One who wanted to just be with her, who would take care of her in every way. She looked at the bed. "In every way," she said softly.

Stepping away from the door, she pushed the handsome stranger out of her mind. Picking up the box, she set it and the small tote on the bed. As she went through everything and got organized for the following morning, her fruit salad arrived. When she finished, she climbed into bed, set the alarm, and crashed.

As she dressed the next morning, she called down for breakfast in her room. There wasn't time to go to the restaurant and eat, and she was sure there would be too many people. These events brought hundreds of people out. After she ate, she called someone to help her carry everything to the convention center.

Her table was between Kathy and Sue's, so the three of them could spend the day visiting and watching each other's spaces during bathroom breaks and while each of them walked around to their favorite authors. She loved these things. They were always busy, and it was so much fun to meet fans of her work.

As she started to set up her table, Kathy and Sue finally came. "You ready for this day?" Kathy asked.

"Not sure I am. You should have seen how many people were waiting to get in." She looked at Mel. "Hey, where were you for breakfast?"

"I didn't sleep well, so I just had breakfast in my room. But we are all here now, and then tonight, we can relax and have some fun."

Kathy laughed. "I am so getting drunk."

Mel laughed. "What time do you fly out tomorrow?"

"Not until one. I made sure I got a later flight home. Last year, seven in the morning came too early. I swear I was still drunk when I got on that plane."

They all laughed. When the task of setting up was finally finished, Kathy said she was going to wander around. They still had a good forty minutes until the doors opened to the public.

Sue sat there, looking at Mel. "I'm here if you need to talk."

"I'm good. Really, I am. Sometimes, I forget to keep it closed away in my mind, and it gets away from me. But, honestly, I'm good."

"I couldn't imagine living through something like that."

"I know, and I am grateful for all the conversations we had the months after. But, honestly, spending eighteen months on my own, not talking to anyone and just being with me, someone I think I lost somewhere, was good."

Sue got up and hugged her. "I love you."

Mel hugged her back. "I love you."

Kathy came back. "Well, you girls ready? They are getting ready to open the doors."

Sue and Mel both laughed.

CHAPTER THREE

KARL

Karl was in the dining room most of the early morning, waiting to see if she came down. He sat and watched her two friends eat their breakfast, always looking at the door to see if she was coming. A few times, he noticed that one of them would pick up her phone and text. But she didn't show up. He was getting worried about her, which he found odd. He never cared about anyone except his family, and he was sure that those feelings weren't like this.

Finally, he gave up. Knowing the event had already begun, he slowly made his way into the convention center. The noise was incredible. It was as if everyone in the place was talking at the same time, he was sure he had never heard such a thing. As he slowly moved through the crowd, he noticed there were half-dressed men, banners of half-naked men, and women squealing all over the place.

He browsed as if he was interested, chatted with a few of the authors. Mostly, he watched the people around him. It was a madhouse, to say the least. As he made his way through, he saw a banner with her name on it. There wasn't a half-naked man on it, but instead a soft, sexy couple in a very intimate embrace, their lips nearly touching but not. There were no other words except for her name in very unobtrusive lettering, in a soft purple color. She was between her two friends whose banners were a bit sexier.

As he looked around, almost all the banners displayed were hot, sexy, blunt. But not hers. She stood out in the crowd in that aspect. Somehow, he believed she stood out tremendously next to her peers. Casually, he made his way down the row of tables, slowly moving toward hers, when he saw her stand. He was close enough to hear her tell her friend that she would be back in a few minutes, that she needed to grab something to eat.

He watched her put her bag across her body and then move away from her table. He didn't follow her; although, he wanted to. He wanted to talk to her again, maybe have a real conversation, but he just kept moving down the line. When he finally reached her table, he stood there, shocked at what he saw. Counting mentally, there were sixteen books on the table displayed for everyone to see. Behind each book were stacks of that book. *Is that what was in the bag she was pulling?* His eyes fell on bookmarks and a bunch of other things.

"Is there something I can help you with?" her friend asked.

Karl looked up at her, smiling. "Are these your books?" He knew they weren't.

He heard her take a deep breath when he looked up at her. She smiled big. "No, these are Mel Cross's books. Are you a model?"

"No, not a model. Just a normal guy."

"Well, you should be a model. You could make a great deal of money. You're gorgeous."

Karl chuckled. "Thank you, but," he nodded toward her banner, "I think I'm a bit old for that."

Kathy turned around to look at her banner. "No, you're not too old."

His eyes moved to Mel's banner. "Hers is a bit tame compared to the rest."

Kathy laughed. Standing, she moved closer to him. "Mel's stories aren't as forthcoming as most."

"What does that mean exactly?" He was curious now.

"Have you read any of her books?"

"No."

"Well, Mel's stories will rip your heart out. Make sure you have a box of tissues when you read them. She has a gift with words and can make you feel every emotion her characters feel. You feel as if you are standing in the room with them, living life with them. It's a hard thing to do. I mean, we all do it, but I think with Mel, her stories are more life-based, where as ours, well, mine anyway, is fantasy based. I mean, how real is it to expect to meet the man of your dreams in an elevator? How real is that you meet a guy in a hotel bar, have sex with him, and then become life partners? It's not, and if it is, then it's a one in a million chance."

Karl stood there looking at this woman, wondering what the hell kind of world these people lived in. He was exactly that, the fantasy guy, but his fantasy came with a price, a very high price. Every dream a woman had ever thought to dream, he could make them come true.

"Oh, here comes Mel now."

Karl turned his head to see her walking over. He didn't feel so comfortable when a shirtless guy walked up to her, grabbed her in a hug, and lifted her off the ground. He stood there watching the exchange of words and nodding of their heads, and then she turned and headed away from the shirtless guy, toward him. She stopped a few steps from him.

"Well, hello again." She smiled at him.

Karl nodded. "Hello."

She moved behind her table, putting her bag down. "So, are you a fan or a writer?"

He laughed. "Neither, just curious. Wait, that came out wrong. Yes, I'm a person who reads. I wasn't aware you were a writer, so not really a fan, but I could be persuaded. No, not a writer, but I do have a hell of a story to tell. There, how was that?"

She laughed. "Not bad. So what do you read? What kinds of books?"

"I like a good mystery, but your friend here was telling me about your books."

Karl watched as she looked at her friend. "Was she now?"

"She was. I read in the pamphlet that you have a new book out."

Her eyes glared up at him. He felt as if he was about to be scolded, but he didn't look away. "Yes."

"Well, then I think I'd like to get a copy of it."

Her grin was slow-moving. Picking up a copy of the book, she opened the cover. "Who should I make out to?"

"Karl, with a K," he smarted.

"Okay, Karl with a K." She was writing, then she closed the book and handed it to him. "For the help last night."

"Oh, no, let me pay you."

"Your money is no good here. You were kind enough to help me out last night, and trust me, if I had dropped that box, I would have spent at least a few hours trying to organize everything in it. Please, just take the book, Karl with a K."

He reached forward, taking the book from her hand. "Thank you."

Turning, he went to walk away, but stopped, picking up a bookmark. "So I don't lose my place."

She nodded to him with a smirk on her lips. "No, we can't have that, now can we?"

"Nope." He walked away.

Mel

When he was far enough away, Sue leaned over. "What the hell was that about?"

Kathy chimed in. "You know, if I wasn't married, I would have been all over him. Shit, he was fucking gorgeous. Did you see those eyes? Who the hell has eyes that blue?"

Mel just laughed. "He helped me carry in my box of swag last night."

Sue looked at her. "And why didn't you invite him to your room?"

"Come on, guys. You know I'm not interested. Look at the past three years of my life. I am in no way, shape, or form in the mood to deal with anything other than myself. Go flirt. Who's going to tell? Not me." They all laughed.

Karl

As Karl walked away, he itched to turn around to see if she was watching him, but he didn't. He took his book and left the venue, heading back to his room. He couldn't wipe the smile off his face. She was funny and witty, liked to banter, something none of the women he dated were.

Lying on his bed, he pulled out his reading glasses and opened the book. The inscription read:

Karl with a K,
Thank you for your chivalry. Enjoy.
Mel Cross

His smile broadened. "Chivalry. Imagine that." For some reason, he felt a bit of pride within himself. His mother would definitely be proud to hear that. Although he lived his life in an unconventional way, programmed to be polite and courteous, a gentleman, he never thought of himself as chivalrous.

Opening the book, he read the dedication.

For you, my love. For teaching me how to be me. For loving me, uncondi-tionally, and for making me take the time to breathe. I love you. You will hold my heart in your hands until it's our time again.

His fingers moved across the words, wondering what it meant. He'd looked at her hand and didn't see a ring, nor did it look like there was a ring mark. Setting the book down, he pulled out his phone and pulled up Google, typing in her name. He found her web page and her Facebook account. He wasn't on Facebook, so he couldn't look at it. He went to her web page.

As he read, he discovered who her love was. She was a mother, but there was no mention of a husband. Putting his phone down, he picked up the book and read the dedication again. He placed his hand on the page. Closing his eyes, he let the words run through his mind. For whatever reason, he felt sadness fill his heart. Sliding his hand down the page, he opened his eyes, turned the page over, and began to read.

Hours later, after becoming so involved in her words, in her story, he realized he was late to the ball. He didn't bother showering because there wasn't time. Hurrying to get dressed, Karl grabbed his mask and headed down to the convention center, which had now been transformed into an elegant space. Tables were set, there were two bars, and music played at a moderate volume.

Women were dressed to the nines in formal gowns and beautiful masks. He was going to have a hell of a time finding her. Deciding to walk around for a bit to get a feel for the place, he watched women checking him out, which he found a bit unnerving. Models walking around without shirts.

He found a table laid out with food, so he placed a few finger foods on a plate—he hadn't eaten since breakfast—and found himself a place against the wall out of the way. His mind was still stuck on her words, on the emotions she'd managed to pull to the surface of his being. She was gifted, talented, and one hell of a writer. As he stood there watching the hundreds of people, he realized finding her here would be as difficult as finding a needle in a haystack. He decided to casually walk around when the lights dimmed, and the music got a bit louder. People were moving toward the dance floor, and that's when he saw her. Her hair was up with ringlets of curls hanging down, the grey streaks giving her appearance away.

She was wearing a long, black, form-fitting dress, showing off her full but so sexy figure. He wouldn't call her fat by any means. Healthy was the word he would choose. She was stunning. He stood in the shadows and watched her for a minute until the music changed to a slower tune. Before she had the chance to move off the dance floor, he stepped up behind her. "May I have this dance?" he asked softly.

When she turned to look at him, a smile lit up her face. She looked at his hand, which he held out and waited patiently for her to take. She slowly lifted her hand, and when she placed it in his, he gently closed his fingers around it. He placed his other hand on her waist, and she rested hers on his shoulder. He wanted to pull her close to his body, but he didn't know her, so he held her at a respectable distance. Chivalrous. He smiled.

"Hello, Karl with a K."

He chuckled. "Hello, Miss Cross. How was your day?"

She giggled. "It was quite successful. Thank you."

"Well then, that would be a good day."

"One of the better. But, then again…" She stopped talking.

Karl felt her body tense. "We should celebrate." He wanted to change the subject.

"And how would we do that?"

"We could have a celebratory drink."

She looked him in the eye. "I don't drink."

"We could go for a walk and talk, or we could just stay here and dance."

She didn't say anything, so he just kept dancing with her. When the music ended, she took a step back and let her arm slide off his shoulder. With her other hand still in his, she smiled at him.

"Thank you for the celebratory dance, Karl. If you'll excuse me, I think it's time for me to get some sleep. You have a lovely evening." She slipped her fingers from his hand and turned to walk away.

He reached out to touch her arm, and she stopped, turning to look at him. "Will you go for a walk with me? I'd like to have a conversation with you." She stood there for a long time, just looking at him. He could see her struggling, could see the warring in her eyes. "Don't say no." He had stepped closer, bending his head to whisper in her ear. It felt as if all eyes in the room were watching them, the music still playing in the background. The murmur in the room grew softer. They were on display, which made him feel a bit uncomfortable, but their masks left them anonymous. However, everyone in the room knew who she was. Only she knew who he was, and she didn't even know that yet.

She rose, pushing up on her toes to reach his ear. "Please, don't do this. It's not something you want to do. I'm damaged. I'm afraid the scars are deep, and the wound is even deeper."

His eyes locked on hers as she lowered herself. He couldn't help himself. He leaned in and kissed her on the forehead. Tilting his head, resting his forehead on hers, he whispered, "No one is beyond repair." When he pulled his head away, he watched as her eyes filled with tears. He wanted nothing more than to pull her into his arms and hold her. But she pulled away, turning, he let her go and watched her walk toward the exit. His eyes never left her back until the door closed behind her. When he looked around, people were standing there looking at him. The only sound was the music in the background. *Fuck.* He nodded and walked away. As he moved through the room, the chatter began again. When he walked out the door, pulling his mask off, he searched the space for her. But he knew he wouldn't see her. He knew she was gone.

CHAPTER FOUR

MEL

Mel couldn't believe the way this man made her feel. From the moment she touched his hand, she felt a calm come over her. The dance made her feel like she was in some sort of trance. He was so kind, as if he knew the pain she felt, the pain that wouldn't allow her to feel anything but that. Moving away from him wasn't as easy as she wanted to believe it would be. That morning at her signing table, she felt an attraction to him then. Her feet moved against her will. She believed she would like to walk with him, talk with him. But men did nothing but disappoint her. People disappointed her. Hell, life disappointed her.

She made it to the elevators just as she heard the doors in the hall open, the noise and music getting louder. When she turned in the elevator before she pushed the button, she looked up to see him pull his mask off and turn his head toward her. She moved to stand to the side so he couldn't see her, and the doors closed. Pulling her mask off, she wiped her eyes and pushed the button to her floor. "What the fuck?" When the doors opened, she rushed down the hall to her room. Leaning against the door as she shut it, the tension left her in the solitude. It's where she felt the best. After a few deep breaths, she moved about the room, changing her clothes, and packing up her event things and suitcase. It was her birthday week, and she was going to the beach. A few hours later, she took her event things to her car. On her way back to the front door, she found herself walking toward the water. She loved the beach. The ocean felt so much better to her, but water was water. The serenity and solitude she felt near it were undeniable.

When she hit the sand, her shoes came off her feet, and she moved toward the water. Sitting down, she pushed her feet into the sand, wrapped her arms around her legs, and propped her chin on her knees. In her heart, she knew she was broken. She hoped that when it was all over, she would feel at peace, but peace was the furthest thing from her heart. After sitting there for some time, she pushed up and turned to go back to her room, when she was caught up by the man standing a few feet from her, looking at her. She smiled. "I'm sorry about earlier."

"No, don't be sorry. If anyone should be sorry, it's me."

She looked at him. His voice was kind, his eyes sincere. Not knowing what to say, she just stood there looking at him. When he took a step forward, she shook her head. "Please." Licking her lips, she continued. "I should go." She turned, picked up her shoes, and started walking back to the hotel.

"Mel," he said, his voice close to her.

She stopped and turned. "My name isn't Mel. That's just the name I write under. My name is Laney, but no one here knows that. No one knows who I am. They only know what I want them to know. No one knows me. The only one who did is…" She stopped talking and swallowed hard. "My name is Laney." She nodded and turned to walk away.

"Please, don't go. Come and walk with me. We don't need to talk."

"What makes you think I want to walk?"

"I'm not sure, but I would like it if you would keep me company. I mean, it's a bit creepy out here, and I am all alone." He smiled at her.

She tilted her head. "I'm not so sure that's a good idea. I don't know you. What if you are a wolf in sheep's clothing?"

"I won't lie to you; I am very much a wolf, but I don't hide that."

"Well then, by your own admission, it wouldn't be wise of me to go anywhere secluded with you. My fear would eat me alive." She could feel excitement building deep inside, something she never thought she would ever feel again. "Seriously. It wouldn't be a good idea." She turned to walk away.

"I've been a citizen of this country for seven years. Just a random fact about me."

As she stepped away, she turned her head. "I've never owned a dresser. Just a random fact about me. Goodnight, Karl."

"Will you be here tomorrow?"

"Yes, I leave on Monday," she called out as she slipped her shoes on.

"Have a meal with me."

She laughed, shaking her head as she made her way into the hotel.

Karl

Karl watched her walk away. She was sassy, and that excited him. He was having a difficult time with the reasoning in his mind. He never spent this much energy on gaining the attention of a woman. But, then again, there hadn't been a woman who interested him this much. He was just grateful she wasn't the job.

Turning, he headed back to the water's edge. Looking out, the only thing he could think about was his mother, and how he was disrespecting her by throwing away the values she'd taught him. She'd taught him to respect women, all women. He was courteous, yes. He was polite, yes. But he didn't give a shit about any of them, and that made him an arrogant asshole. But this woman, he turned to look at the hotel, this woman drew him to her like a magnet, pulling him toward her. He was convinced that, no matter what he did, even if he was to get in his car and drive away right now, he would regret not trying to know her. Even if nothing came of it, even if they just became friends. It felt important, vital that she become some part of his life. Somehow, he needed her.

He heard people talking and knew his solidarity was no longer, so he headed back to the hotel. The voices were attached to a few of the women from the event. As he approached them, one of them looked up at him.

"Are you a model?" Her words were a bit slurry.

He smiled. "No, ma'am, not a model." His eyes moved along the length of her body. She was rocking the gown she had on. The slit along the side of her dress revealed her tan, toned thigh. When his eyes traveled back up her body to her face, she had her bottom lip tucked between her teeth.

"Like something you see?"

He knew what the next line was in this cat and mouse game. He knew it would take one sentence for him to get laid. But she was just another face covered in makeup. Her hair, even though it looked lovely, was full of hairspray. It wasn't what he wanted. Two days ago, he would have had this woman pinned to a wall and naked within fifteen minutes. Smiling, he was kind with his words. "I'm sure I am not the man for you. I don't feel worthy of such beauty. You ladies have a lovely evening." He nodded at her, making sure he didn't insult her.

She giggled as he moved away from them. Entering the hotel, he happened to notice Laney sitting in the little café across from the restaurant. She was bobbing a tea bag up and down in her cup. Smiling, his body just moved toward her. As he approached her table, she looked up from her tablet and smiled. "Can I join you?" She smirked at him and nodded slightly. Karl smiled as he pulled out the chair across from her. A waitress came over to take his order. "May I ask what you are reading?"

She closed her tablet, slipping it into her bag. "A manuscript for a book."

"Is it your book? One you wrote?"

He watched as she picked up her cup with red-colored liquid in it. Slowly, she brought it to her lips. He moaned lowly when he realized he wanted to be that cup. Gently, she blew on the liquid and then took a small sip. Her eyes were locked on his as he watched her.

As she set her cup back down, she said, "Yes. Can I ask you a question?"

He chuckled. "I'm finding that anything you have to say is something I believe I want to hear. So, yes, you can ask me a question, or two or three. Hey, I've got an idea. Why don't we just have a conversation?"

Her smile, he noticed, was slow, but God it was stunning. "What is it that you hope to gain by this?"

He sat there for a few minutes, just looking at her. He couldn't judge her age, but she wasn't as young as the women he had been with, the women who paid for his time. He realized it didn't matter to him. The waitress set his cup down and looked at Laney. "Can I get you some more hot water?"

"That would be great. Thank you."

Picking up his cup, he put it to his lips, taking a sip of the hot coffee. As he set his cup down, he leaned forward a bit, his eyes locking with hers. The color fascinated him. "I'm not sure I understand the question."

She closed the gap between them, across the small table, her face inches from his. In a soft whisper, she told him, "I'm not going to sleep with you, if that's what you think is going to happen here."

He couldn't resist. "Well, let me just put this out there. If it ever came to that place, trust me, there would be no sleeping, at least until I've had my fill of you, and you of me."

That sparked genuine laughter from her, and she leaned back against her chair. "Something I've heard many times in my life. A fable. I find that men believe themselves to be that man. The idea of a man being that to or with a woman is the crap we write about, fantasy, complete and utter hope. But, in my experience, that's all it is. A scene in a story made up in our minds. Oh, Karl with a K, thank you for the giggle."

He was amazed at her ability to challenge him, with her smart and witty mouth. He leaned back in his chair, putting his hands on his thighs, and watched her pick up her cup and drink whatever was in it. The waitress walked over and set a little teapot of hot water on the table. "Thank you," she said. She drained her cup and reached for her bag, pulling out a red and green tea bag. She carefully opened it up and put the bag in her cup, and then poured the water in. She put her elbow on the table, resting her chin on her hand as she bobbed the tea bag up and down. Her eyes moved to his, a smile on her face.

Leaning forward, he mimicked her. "In some instances, your made-up stories, your fantasies are real."

"I'm not a twenty-year-old woman with high expectations and selfish behaviors who believes the egos of men."

"No, I don't suppose you are."

She let go of her tea bag, picked up her bag, then stood and leaned over to make sure she was close to his ear. "Random fact about me: I've been responsible for my own orgasms for twenty-five years. That's how I know it to be fantasy and not fact." Standing, she smiled at him and said, "Goodnight, Karl."

He stood and turned, watching her walk out, his smile hurting his cheeks. He took off after her, trotting up behind her as she waited for the elevator. "Random fact about me: I don't know how to sew."

Laughing, she turned her head to look up at him. "Good to know." The doors opened, and she stepped forward. When she turned around, her smile still graced her lips. "Well? Are you coming?"

Karl stepped into the elevator. "I'm not going to sleep with you."

She giggled. "Good, then you aren't going to be disappointed when I don't invite you to my room."

He leaned in from behind her to whisper in her ear. "I would never go to a hotel room with you. I wouldn't cheapen the experience like that."

The doors opened, and she stepped forward. He watched as she put her hand on the door. When she turned, the fire in her eyes made his heart speed up. "I'm not a rude or mean person by nature. I don't appreciate the innuendo. I am so much more than a tawdry affair. I can assure you, Karl with a K, that I have no interest in anything to do with you. You seem to forget, I'm the one who keeps walking away. I get the want what you can't have game, and I'm sure you feel the need to pursue, to fulfill whatever kind of internal score card you keep, but I'm not that girl." Her words were hard, cold, and to the point. Her hand moved off the door, and she stepped back.

He was stunned by her words, not discouraged but impressed. He knew for sure that he needed to have this woman in his life. The door closed. He jumped forward, hitting the door open button, but it didn't open. She was on the fifth floor, and he was on the ninth. Pushing the button for the sixth floor, the doors opened, and he ran out, looking for the stairs. Down the stairs, he ran. Whipping the door open, he ran out into the hallway. He heard her door close, so he headed down the hall, listening as he went. As he moved down the hallway, he could hear televisions, kids playing, and people snoring. Then he heard her voice. "Yes, this is room five eighteen. I would like to order a fruit salad. Thank you." He stood outside the door for a few minutes, getting his nerve to knock. Was he stalking her? No, he wasn't. This was him apologizing for over stepping. He paced back and forth in front of her door, looking at it as he passed it each time. He wasn't sure what he would say or how he would apologize to her for being such an asshole.

"Only one way to do this." His hand reached up, and he gently knocked on the door.

When she opened it, her face changed from a small smile to a tight-lipped look. "Why are you doing this? Please, just leave me alone." She went to push the door closed. He did the one asshole move he knew, putting his hand on the door.

"Please, five minutes. I am so sorry for being an asshole. You are right; the innuendo was so out of line. My mother didn't raise that man. I cannot say how sorry I am. I get it, and please, I just need you to understand that I realize I was being an arrogant asshole. I just want to get to know you, and yes, comments like that are uncalled for."

She shook her head. "Why me? What, there aren't enough young, skinny women out there for you to harass?"

"When I saw you in the restaurant the other morning, there was just something that touched me here." He put his hand on his chest. "I can feel it. I just want to get to know you. I don't expect anything. Just two people becoming friends."

She stood there for a long time, looking at him. "I'm leaving the day after tomorrow. What is the point?"

"I don't know what the point would be. I just know that I will regret not trying to get to know you. Just say yes to maybe spending the day with me tomorrow. I mean, if you're leaving, then what difference would it make? It would just be a wonderful day spent with a potentially new friend. A new fan."

Someone cleared their throat. Karl turned to see a man standing there with a tray in his hands. Laney smiled, taking the tray and thanking him. Looking at Karl, she smiled. "Fine, but no more innuendo."

"No more innuendo. Breakfast?"

"I have plans for breakfast with my friends, but after is fine. I'll meet you in the lobby."

He nodded and turned, walking back down to the elevator. He returned to his room, changed, and grabbed her book. Getting comfortable, he continued reading.

CHAPTER FIVE

Laney sat on her bed with her fruit salad, looking at her door. She was unnerved by his brazen approach to her. But, then again, she hadn't had a man pursue her in two decades, hell, nearly three. What she couldn't figure out was why a man that good looking wanted to know her. She got up and went to the bathroom to look at herself in the mirror. Her hair was greying; that's why she had the streaks put in, so it wasn't obvious. Her wrinkles were visible, especially around her mouth and her eyes. Turning her head to look at her profile, she shook her head. "What the hell does he see? Why would he want to be with me?"

Clicking off the light, she went back to her bed and picked up her tablet, deciding not to worry about it. She was leaving on Monday, and he was right. It wouldn't matter. There was no way she was sleeping with him. But, then again, he was gorgeous. She looked down at her body; she was by no means thin or firm. Hell, she had her body stuffed into Spanx and a corset to hold everything in. After losing a hundred and twenty-six pounds, she was saggy all over. She giggled at the fact that when she took her fantastic bra off, her boobs, well, they were just sacks of flesh with nipples on them. She just couldn't understand why a man who looked like him would want anything to do with her. Tossing her tablet on the bed, she grabbed her sweater and key card and headed downstairs. She needed some fresh air.

Standing on the beach, looking out at the water, she was trying to decide if she should just leave right now and head to the beach at the ocean. There was no way she wanted to play this game with this man. She knew he was way out of her league and that she was just setting herself up for a huge disappointment. He was so pretty, and she was lacking human contact and the touch of a man. But for the last fifteen years, she'd longed for the touch of a man, one that was more than five minutes of very forgettable sex. Hell, she couldn't remember the last time she had an actual kiss, a deep, passionate, jaw-dropping kiss. Shaking her head, she knew she had to leave for her own self-preservation. With her mind made up, she turned to go back to the hotel to check out and get her things. She would send Sue and Kathy a text saying goodbye and that she would see them next month in New York.

When she looked up, he was standing there, watching her. "I feel terrible," he said softly to her.

"You shouldn't. I told you I'm damaged goods. I can't do this with you. I don't want to do this. I'm leaving tonight instead of Monday."

"I understand. I didn't mean to scare you, and I know I'm the one who is going to regret this."

"You didn't scare me; you made me think. I'm the one who scared me. Listen, this," she moved her hand up and down her body, "isn't something you want. I don't have a hard body. Hell, I don't even have a nice body. I'm held together with Spanx and a hell of a good bra. You would only be disappointed, and in turn, would disappoint me. I've been alone for a long time. Random fact: I've spent the last eighteen months alone, speaking to no one. Not one word. This outing was my first in nearly three years. I think I may have taken a bigger step than I was ready for."

"Laney, believe it or not, it was not my intention to pursue you for a sexual relationship, but to be honest with you after that dance, the thought crossed my mind. But it wasn't my intention. I just feel this pull toward you. I can't explain it without sounding like some kind of idiot trying to convince you to go to bed with me."

"Well, thank you, but I don't think this is a good idea. It was really nice to meet you, and thank you for the dance. You seem like a very lovely man, and I hope you find what it is you're looking for in this life."

She moved around him and headed back to the hotel. Stopping when she hit the pavement, she blinked her eyes. Her heart sped up, and her stomach rolled over. Standing twenty feet from her was the last person on the planet she expected to see. He stood there looking at her, and her first instinct was to turn around, so she did. Her feet were moving back to Karl, but was that the wisest thing for her to do? She stopped and just stood there, her eyes filling with tears. She didn't want to do this. She made the break. She signed the papers and left. This was her life now, not his, not hers with him, but hers.

Karl stood there, looking at her from about five feet away. "Are you all right?" he asked softly.

She slowly shook her head as the first tear fell on her cheek. That's when she heard him. "Laney? Laney, is that you?" His voice sounded closer than it should have been. Her eyes locked on Karl's. She didn't know why, but for some reason, she wanted him to save her, but she also knew he couldn't. This was her problem; this *was* her life.

When his hand touched her shoulder, her whole body cringed away from him. "Don't."

"Baby, where the hell have you been? You just disappeared into thin air. The second I heard you were going to be here, I came."

"I signed the papers. I don't want this with you anymore. Why are you doing this?"

"You're my wife. I love you. I don't understand why you would run away. We had a wonderful life. Come on, let's go talk." He wrapped his fingers gently around her arm. "What have you done to yourself? Your hair, your body, it's so different. You look beautiful. I don't know about the dark hair. I told you I prefer blonde, but it's all right. We can talk about that as well. There's a restaurant in there. We can talk in there. I've got a room, or we can share yours."

She pulled her arm away from him, her eyes still on Karl's, and he looked confused. When her eyes closed and the tears fell, her breath stopped when she felt Karl slip between her and her husband. "Excuse me, would you please not touch my girlfriend?"

Karl snaked his arm around her, pulling her against his back. He wasn't a small man, so she disappeared behind him.

"Your what? That's my wife. Laney, tell him." There was silence. She was holding her breath. "Wait a minute. Are you in a relationship with her?" She felt her fingers slowly bunch the material that covered his back, pulling herself closer to him.

"Listen, I don't know who you are, but she apparently doesn't want to talk to you. Why don't you just walk away?"

"I'm not walking away. I've been looking for her for nearly two years. Laney, please come and talk to me."

She shook her head against Karl's back. "The lady doesn't wish to talk to you. Why don't you go chill out? Maybe tomorrow will be a better day?"

"I don't know who you are, but that is my wife," he shouted.

Laney stepped out from behind Karl. "I am not your wife. I signed the papers nearly two years ago. I left because I don't want to be with you anymore. I just want my life. Go home, Don. Go home. Forget about me. Go be a father and a grandfather. Just leave me alone."

Don stood there looking at Karl then her. "Why would you cheat on me? You promised when we said our vows that you would never cheat on me."

Turning, she looked at Karl, her eyes pleading with him. "Please, get me out of here." Her voice was so soft.

"You got it," he whispered, his fingers touching her tear-streaked face. He pulled her to his chest. Looking at Don, he said, "Please, excuse us." Laney felt him moving them. Then he stopped, let her go, and stepped in front of her. "Listen, I don't know what the hell is going on here, but the lady is obviously upset, so why don't you go take a breather and let her calm down? I'm sure, when she calms down, she will come and talk to you. What room are you in?"

"Six-twelve," Don answered.

Karl nodded to him and turned, placing his hand on the small of her back and walking her back to the hotel. He escorted her to the elevators, and when they entered, he pushed the button for his floor. Laney stood there, looking at the buttons. "I'm on five."

"I know you are, but I think you need to talk to someone, and we don't know if he knows what room you're in."

She felt herself move and push the button for the fifth floor. "I can't stay here. I have to leave. Would you walk me to my car, please? I can't see him."

"Of course."

Once in her room, she put her things in her bag and looked at him. "Thank you. I don't even know what to say to you but thank you." He reached up to touch her face, but she stepped back. "We should go." She moved around him to the door.

Karl stood there, looking at the desk. Picking up a pen, he wrote his personal phone number down. Turning, he handed it to her. "Please, let me know when you get wherever it is that you are going."

She looked at the paper. Taking it from him, she slipped it into her bag. She knew she was never going to use it, but he was kind to her, and she needed kindness right now. She needed to be protected. It's not in the sense that Don would cause her any physical harm; he wasn't like that. She just couldn't stand to see his pain or hear his excuses or promises anymore. She was done being responsible for someone else. She was done taking care of people. It was just her. Looking up at Karl, her hand moved to his incredible lips, her fingers gently touching them. His eyes looked into her soul; at least, that's how she felt. Pulling her hand back, she turned, and they left her room. She took him out a side exit closer to her car.

He opened her door for her. "Please, be safe." His words were soft, his eyes softer.

"I will. Thank you, Karl, for noticing me. It's been a long time since someone has seen me. Have a good life. I hope you find everything it is you are looking for." She got in the car, and he closed her door.

He stood there completely numb. He had never felt so helpless in his life. Watching her car pull away, he noticed the Mississippi plates. His fingers moved to his lips, where her touch had seared them. Who was this woman, and what the hell was the attraction, the pull he felt? Turning, he headed back in and went straight to the man's room. His knock was a bit harder than he intended, but he was pissed. Don opened the door.

"She's gone, I just watched her pull out of the parking lot. Care to tell me what is going on?" Don opened the door, inviting him in. Karl checked him out. He looked like an old man, thin and bald. His eyes were swollen and puffy. Don sat in the chair and crossed his legs like a woman would.

"She signed divorce papers, sold our home, and walked out. I've been looking for her ever since. I don't know how many of these fucking book events I've been to, looking for her. None of her family has heard from her, and if they have, they haven't told me a fucking thing. Her granddaughter hasn't heard from her in over a year, and that's not like her. For the longest time, I thought she was dead. Then I saw she was speaking here, so I got in the car and drove down."

"How long were you married?"

"What are you talking about? We are still married. I didn't sign the papers, and I'm not going to, so you are sleeping with a married woman."

Karl laughed. "I'm not sleeping with her. I just met her two days ago."

"You said she was your girlfriend."

"I had no idea who you were, and she looked terrified. What did you expect me to do? How long?"

"Well, it would have been our seventeenth anniversary last month. I don't understand why she left. Did she say anything to you?"

Karl looked at him. "I told you I just met her. I know her name isn't Mel Cross; that's the name she writes under. I know her name is Laney and she drinks some kind of red tea. That's about it."

"Well, she looks totally different. Her hair used to be blondish-red, and she weighed a hell of a lot more than she does now. She looks good."

"I just wanted to tell you that she left. I'm sorry, but I think you should sign the papers and move on. It's obvious that she doesn't want to be with you."

"Why, so you can move in?"

Karl laughed. "The fact that you are still married to her isn't going to make a difference to me or anyone else. But that's not who I am with her. We are just friends, nothing more. You have a good life. I'm going to bed. I have a plane to catch in the morning."

"Are you one of those models?"

He laughed. "Nope, not a model. Goodnight." He walked out and went to his room. Lying on his bed holding her book, his eyes closed as his fingers touched his lips. He didn't think he would ever be the same. Opening the book to his bookmarked place, he began reading. Hours later, he closed the book, feeling that he knew a bit more about her. She was a very deep feeling woman. There was no way in the world that just any woman could write words like this. Her friend was right; she pulled him in, and now she had a fan for life. When he got home, he was going to order all her books. He dropped his clothes and climbed into bed. Turning off the light, he lay in complete darkness. His phone lit up the room. Picking it up, he had a text message from an unknown number. Swiping it over, the words jumped off the stark white background.

~I'm safe. Pulled into a hotel down the road. Too upset to drive. Thank you again. ~

His chest tightened. He had her number now. After saving it in his phone, he texted back.

~Glad to hear you are being sensible. You never have to thank me for anything. ~

Smiling, he hit send. Turning it on vibrate, he laid it on his chest. He hoped she felt what he did, the pull. When it vibrated, he sat up.

~It would be rude to not say thank you. I'm going to be fine. Please, go on with your life. Don't give me a backward glance. ~

~Well, there's the problem. I wouldn't turn my back on you in the first place. I'm heading home tomorrow, back to my real life. ~

~Oh? As opposed to the fake one you share with me? ~

He laughed. "If you only knew."

~Nothing I shared with you was fake. I was here on business. Should have left the morning I saw you in the restaurant. ~

~Okay, so now you've piqued my curiosity. Why didn't you leave? ~

"Because of you." *~I met someone. ~*

~Oh. ~

"Yeah, oh." *~Stay safe, Laney. I hope one day we will meet again. ~*

~Why's that, Karl with a K? ~

~Because I believe you are someone I want to know better. Someone I believe I need in my life. ~

~Goodnight, Laney. ~

He waited for a response until his phone went dark. With a smile on his face, he closed his eyes, holding his phone to his chest. But it didn't vibrate, and it didn't light up. Even when he woke the next morning, there was nothing. The screen was blank except for his words.

CHAPTER SIX

Laney decided just to head down to the beach. It wasn't that far of a drive. She checked into a hotel since her rental wouldn't be ready until Monday. When she walked into her room, she opened the sliding doors to hear the waves as they lapped against the shore. Sitting down, she pulled out the pack of cigarettes she bought when she stopped to get gas and lit one up. She hadn't had a smoke in nearly two years, but her nerves were shot, and she needed something to comfort her. She didn't want it to be food, not after everything she'd done to lose all the weight. Three smokes later, she got up and took a shower, and then crawled into bed with her bag. She had a manuscript to read, and fucking Don was not going to derail her. He wouldn't find her here, and he wouldn't find her in Mississippi. She had sold her car, changed her appearance, and now lived the exact life she wanted. When she pulled out her tablet, a piece of paper slipped onto her lap. Her smile was automatic as she picked it up to see his name and number. "Should I?" Picking up her phone, she sent a text, not expecting him to respond since it was going on one in the morning. A few minutes later, his words stunned her.

~*Because I believe you are someone I want to know better. Someone I believe I need in my life.* ~

~Goodnight, Laney. ~

She sat there looking at her phone. "What? Why would he say that?" She couldn't do anything but look at her phone. "It's too late for this shit." She put her phone on the night table and shut off the light. Maybe in the morning, she would feel better. She didn't even clear off the bed, just closed her eyes and crashed. Monday, she would be in her rental for the week, on the fifteenth floor, where she could just look at the ocean and forget and remember all at the same time. Don wasn't going to have power over her anymore. She was her own person now; someone she had lost but found again.

When morning came, she called to see if she could get in a earlier, then she had breakfast on her way out of the hotel and headed to the grocery store to get her supplies. After getting the keys to the luxurious apartment she had rented for the week, she made herself at home. She changed the sheets and pillowcases, made lunch, then sat on the balcony and let the stress of the last few days go. Her mind was free of everything, including Don and Karl.

Karl woke with his phone in his hand. Picking it up, he swiped it on, but there was no response from her. Admitting to himself that he was disappointed shocked him. He had hoped. But after talking to her husband, he knew she was upset. What he wanted to know was why she left. What would cause a woman to just walk away? He had heard her tell him to go and be a father and a grandfather. Did that mean she had grown children out there? Why would a woman walk away from her own children? But then he remembered that he said they were married for seventeen years. "Maybe the children were his, not hers." She didn't strike him as a cold-hearted woman. As he moved about the room, gathering his things and packing his bag, thoughts of her kept flashing in his mind. Her fingers touched his lips; why did she do that?

Taking his bag, he made his way down to the restaurant to have something to eat, then he headed toward the airport. When he got home, he went to the balcony and stood there looking at his beloved ocean. In his whole life, he had never seen anything more incredible. A childhood dream, his American dream. As he stood there, he felt as if his dream was changing, but that was ridiculous. How could it change? She made it clear that she didn't want any part of him. Was he just being an arrogant asshole, thinking he could get whatever he wanted, take what he wanted? Not with this woman. This was the kind of woman his mother taught him about. The kind of woman who deserved respect, the kind you searched your whole life for.

As he unpacked his bag, he pulled out her book. Looking at the cover, he saw it was a beach scene. He smiled. She definitely deserved every fucking ounce of respect he could give her. He changed and headed to the gym. He'd been gone a few days longer than he expected and hadn't worked out at all. Maybe if he got some endorphins worked up, he would feel like his old self. This person he was right now was ready to quit being a date for hire. Somehow, he knew she wouldn't approve or understand.

Once at the gym, he headed to his office, where he was sure there were massive amounts of paperwork and plenty of clients to talk to. He only hoped everyone did their jobs and covered for him. An hour later, he was pleased that there were no fires to put out, no angry clientele, so now he could just work out for a bit. Leaving his phone on his desk as he always did, he headed out to the weights.

Laney grabbed her tablet. She needed to get through her manuscript and get it to the editor, but she wasn't feeling it. His words still echoed in her mind. She didn't understand why he would say the things he'd said. He couldn't want her like that. She wasn't his type. Men who looked like him weren't interested in women who looked like her. She had to be older than him. Well, he had grey hair, and his skin was weathered, but that could just be from the sun. Picking up her phone, she saw that it was dead. It took her a few minutes to find her charger, and it would take a while for it to charge, so she thought she would go down and sit in the sand.

As she sat, her fingers moved to her necklace. Pulling it from her chest, she fingered the hearts on it. "I miss you," she whispered to herself, "so very much." Putting the chain back into her blouse, she headed back up to the apartment. Picking up her phone, she swiped it on and pulled up his last text. She stood there, staring at it. "What did it mean? What did he mean?"

She started typing.

~Why would you say this to me? I am a stranger. You are a stranger. A beautiful stranger who saved me. What do you think I could possibly give to you that I am sure you don't already have? Please, Karl, I can't do this cat and mouse game with you. ~

She pushed send and went to get something to eat. She was tired and decided to take a nap.

As time moved forward while he worked out, the only thing on his mind was the look on her face when they were on that beach. He wanted to be where she was. He didn't know her name, so he couldn't even find her. He knew her writing name, what state she lived in, and that she was the most real woman he had spoken to in a very long time.

He wasn't paying attention to what was going on around him until a young woman was standing in front of him.

"Hi. You work here, right? That guy over there said you could help me." She pointed to Tom standing across the room.

He smiled at her because he wasn't a rude human. "I can try. What do you need?"

"Well, I'm trying to work on my abs." She lifted her tiny t-shirt to show him her body. "But I'm not so sure the exercise I'm doing is helping. And I see you lifting these weights, along with these incredible abs of yours." Her fingers touched his stomach.

He stood there looking at her, watching what she was doing. When her fingers touched his sweaty skin, he felt nothing. Karl smiled at her, taking her hand from his stomach. "Why don't you show me what you've been doing?"

She pulled her lip between her teeth. "Do you have a girlfriend?"

He laughed. "In fact, I do." Her face said it all; she wanted one thing from him. Sex. It was like this all the time. Every day, women came on to him, all with the same thing on their minds. Sex. Maybe Laney was right. Maybe he wanted something he couldn't have. Maybe the cat and mouse game was what he wanted. Would he still respect her if she gave in and let him have her? He knew he would. She was different, so very different. "Listen, Tom can help you. I have someplace I need to be, so if you'll excuse me." He walked away and walked right to Tom. "Stop sending me these women who want anything other than my help. I pay you to be here, so help her yourself," he snapped.

"What the hell is wrong with you? She asked me if you were available for some fun. Did you see her abs? The chick doesn't need any help. I thought you might want to go a round with her in your office. She seemed willing enough."

Karl turned to look at her, but she was the same as the others— hard, tight body, tits that didn't move when she walked, her nipples hard as rocks poking through her shirt. She actually turned around and bent over so he could see her ass. Shaking his head, he looked at Tom. "No, thanks, I'll pass. You have a good time. I need to go. I think I'm getting sick. Don't burn the place down."

He couldn't do it. He just didn't want to be a part of this right now. Any other day, he would have taken her into his office and fucked the hell out of her, but today, he wanted to feel *her* fingers on his lips. He didn't even bother to shower, just threw on a t-shirt, grabbed his bag and phone, and left.

Slamming the door to his apartment as he walked in, he headed straight to his charger. He was pissed. His phone was dead, and he felt dirty, used, and that wasn't him. He peeled off his clothes as he walked to the shower. Something was happening to him, and he didn't have a fucking clue what it was. Why was he so angry? Women did this to him all the time. It's what he wanted; it's what he always wanted. But now, nearly ten years later, he was done. After his shower, he felt he needed to talk to his mother. Hearing her words of wisdom always made him feel better. She would know how to comfort him, maybe give him some advice on how to move forward with Laney. When he swiped on his phone, he saw her message. His heart sped up as he opened it. Reading her words brought a smile to his face. He didn't text her back, but instead, dialed her number. She didn't answer, so it went to voice mail, but he didn't want to say what he was going to say on voice mail, so he hung up and sent a text.

~I would like to talk to you. ~

When she didn't text back, he called his mother.

"Hello, darling," she said when she answered the phone.

"Hi, Mom."

"How are you? You're usually at work at this time."

"I know. I couldn't work today. I just got back from a trip, and I just don't feel it. Listen, Mom, I need some advice, some of that good old knowledge you've given us over the years."

She laughed. "You've met someone, dear?"

"I think I did. I'm not sure she feels the same about me. I think she does."

"Well, tell me about her."

He laughed. "That's just it. I don't know much about her. She's a writer, a very good writer. That's about it. She is so smart, so quick, and she certainly doesn't think my charms are charming."

"Well, it sounds to me that you might have met your match. Your equal."

"Oh, Mom, she is so far better than I am."

"It's good that you recognize this, then you can be careful with your own ego."

"Mom."

"Oh, please, Karl, I raised you. I know why you moved to America. I know you love women, more so than you should. But if you believe you have found the one who stands out, then I am happy for you. Treat her with care and respect, just like you would your momma."

"Thanks, Mom. I love you."

"I love you, too. Let me know how it goes for you. Does she have a name, this woman who has stolen your heart?"

He smiled. "The world knows her as Mel Cross."

"Mel Cross, the writer? Oh my goodness, I have all of her books. Your father just brought home her new one for me, Everything She Thought. I was just going to start it."

Karl busted out laughing. "I read it this weekend."

"Sweetheart, she is such a deep woman, and the tragedy her poor family suffered… I think it was three years ago. I know you will be good for her. But, honey, isn't she married?"

"No, Mom, not anymore. What tragedy?"

"It was all over the news. It was the reason she stopped writing and disappeared. The press was all over her. Her daughter was home for the summer after finishing medical school. She had a brain aneurism and died in her arms."

His heart stopped. "Oh my God." Karl knew now what the dedication in her book meant.

"Yes, she was a beautiful young woman. She was the top of her class. All of Miss Cross's books are dedicated to her. I think her name was Anna. Karl, she might be a little older than you."

He smiled. "Mom, look at the age difference between you and Dad. Age is a number, that's all."

"Aww, sweetheart, you take extra care with her. I know you date those plastic girls, but you never seem to stay with them long."

"None of them have any depth. This woman called me out on my shit the minute she met me. She challenged me."

"Well, if you end up dating her, bring her so I can meet her. Maybe she'll sign my books for me."

With a smile on his face, he told her, "I will, Mom. I love you, and thanks."

After he disconnected the call, he set his phone on the charger and just stood there. He couldn't imagine what she'd been through. No wonder she spent eighteen months not talking to anyone. He had this overwhelming feeling to just be with her, so she wasn't alone. But he had another phone call to make. He needed to call his boss, Alexander, and quit. It didn't matter anymore how much money he made. These women wanted sex from him, and he wasn't willing to give it to anyone anymore. He had finally reached the end of his career of being a date for hire. Picking up the phone, he dialed the number he never thought he would ever call. After the first ring, he decided that telling him on the phone was a chicken shit move. Alexander had been good to him. He deserved to hear this face to face, so he headed to his office. When he walked in, the receptionist smiled at him.

"Well, hello, Jon. How are you today?"

"Good, and you?"

"Oh, my day just got better. What brings you by the office? You rarely come here." She was Alexander's wife and ran the business with him. She was probably the most plastic woman he had ever met. According to Alexander, she had something like fifteen surgeries to make her look like she was perfection. As he looked at her, Karl realized she pretty much was. She joked about how she had to get a surrogate to have her children because she had no desire to mess with her doctor's creation. She was a lovely woman, but she was as vain as they came, so shallow and more concerned with the way she looked than she was with anything. She knew this was her gravy train to perfection. Hell, Karl wasn't even sure she loved the guy. She was always flirting with the guys.

"I need to see Alexander. Is he in?"

"He sure is, honey. You go ahead on back. I'll buzz him and let him know you're coming."

"Thank you." He walked away. He could see her reflection in the glass as she gawked at him, licking her lips. Shaking his head, he suddenly felt very dirty and very cheap, which shocked the hell out of him because, four days ago, he would have gotten off on it.

After opening the door, Alexander stood and walked around his desk to greet him. "Jon, what brings you by?" They always used their professional names in the office.

"Well, a few things, actually."

"Come, sit. We can talk. Is everything all right?"

Karl sat down. He didn't say anything for a few minutes, just looked at Alexander. "I think it's time for me to leave the company. I don't think I can do this anymore. This last date was my last."

"Did something happen? Was Stephanie out of line? I know she had been a bit forthcoming with Tom. Stalking him."

"No, she was fine. Well, not really, but I handled it. I just can't do this anymore. I feel dirty, cheap. I think I want something more out of life."

Alexander chuckled. "I didn't think you were a lifer. But still, seven years is not a bad run. I understand. I'm glad you came to tell me in person. I'll get you your last paycheck. You know you can come back anytime you want. Did you still want to keep your weekend date?"

"No, I'm going to take a few weeks off and go see my parents. They are getting on in their years. Thank you, Alexander, for everything. If it wasn't for you, I wouldn't have all that I do. It's been great."

Alexander handed him a check. "You are still going to come to our monthly poker games, right?"

Taking the check, Karl laughed. "I wouldn't miss taking your money."

They shook hands, and Karl left the office building. He'd had a good run, all the fucking sex he could ever want, and he was sure he had made nearly a million dollars if not more. But he was done. Meeting Laney made him realize that he might be worth something more. He was an intelligent man, but he never had anyone to talk about things with. The women he dated weren't interested in anything but the event they were at and the sex he might provide after the date was over. He knew, a long time ago, that he wanted more.

His phone vibrated in his pocket as he walked down the street. Pulling it out, he could see it was her. "Hi," he said, happy to be free.

"Why did you call me? Karl, I thought I made it clear that I don't want to do this with you."

"I know, but I can't stop thinking about you, worrying about you. You were pretty upset last night."

"Not so much upset, but more pissed off. I just want to be left alone." Karl wasn't paying attention to the light and walked off the curb, a car laying on the horn as the driver yelled at him. "What are you doing?"

"Nearly getting killed by a crazy cab driver. I'm walking downtown. I was just on my way home. Laney, I read your message, but I don't want to stop this. Not yet. Can't we just get to know one another? I'd like to be your friend. I would like you to be my friend. I think my life needs someone like you."

He heard her take a deep breath. "Go home and call me back. I wouldn't want you to get run over while we are talking. I wouldn't know where to send the ambulance if you got hurt."

He laughed. "Miami. Give me fifteen. Goodbye, Laney.

"Goodbye, Karl."

CHAPTER SEVEN

He made it home in record time, then got comfortable on his bed before dialing her number. "Okay, I am safely tucked away in my bed."

She laughed. "Why do you need someone like me in your life? I'm nothing. Just a writer who writes stories. I've got nothing."

"Well, that's where you are wrong. From that first encounter, you called me out on my shit. No one has ever done that. Well, except for my mom and maybe my brother, but no one ever cared enough to say, 'Hey, Karl, you're being an asshole.'"

"I never called you an asshole."

He laughed. "Not in so many words, no, but you inferred I'm an arrogant asshole. No one has ever done that. You were right, but no one has ever done that."

"So, you are admitting you're an asshole?"

"Oh, sweetheart, arrogant asshole is being kind. I'm also an ego maniac."

She giggled. "Then why in the world would you expect me to want to be friends with you?"

"I'm not sure, but I can and will say this. I don't feel like that when I'm around you. It's as if none of that matters to me anymore. I think I wear that mask to the world because it protects me. You see, deep down inside, I'm a soft-hearted man, and I think if I stay this hardcore wolf, then I can't be hurt." He was telling it all to her. She had a way of making him want to tell all his secrets. She didn't say anything to him. "You still there?" he asked cautiously.

"Yes." Her voice was faint.

"Too much too soon?"

"No. It's just, I don't think any man I know of in the history of the world has ever said something so damning about himself."

He chuckled. "That's the thing; I would never say that to anyone."

"Then why are you saying it to me? Is it lies? Are you just trying to get close to me? You told me you were a wolf; I don't want to know a wolf."

"I am a wolf. I told you I won't tell you things you want to hear. I don't want to be like that anymore. You make me feel like I can tell the truth. You're like a truth serum. I believe I need you in my life. I want you in my life, as my friend. I don't have many of those."

"I find that hard to believe."

"I don't. Everyone wants something from me, and I'm so tired of giving it and getting nothing in return."

"You've seen yourself, right?"

"What you see is what I allow people to see. The attitude, the ego, the arrogance, it's just part of the package, but it's not who I am. I'm just as terrified as the next guy."

"In my experience, which isn't much over the last twenty-four years, guys don't show that. They just don't ever portray themselves as vulnerable. Well, unless, of course, you read romance books."

He laughed. "No, I don't read romance books. But I did finish your book."

She got quiet for a minute. "I don't usually ask, but what did you think?"

Karl heard the shyness in her voice. "It made me cry. Your friend was right."

"My friend?"

"Yes, at the book event. She said that you write so well, you can

50

actually make the reader feel everything the characters in the book are feeling. She said that your talent was miles beyond theirs."

"Well, that was nice of her. I just write what I feel, what the story requires."

"I was in that talk you started to give. I was actually supposed to leave to go see my parents, but I couldn't leave." His voice softened. "Not after seeing you." He almost whispered it.

The pause was long, and she sounded like a scared little girl when she spoke. "Why?"

"I told you. There was just something about you that pulled me in. Without ever saying a word, I just felt you, and I couldn't leave. I knew I would regret it for the rest of my life."

"I shouldn't be doing this with you. I shouldn't be lying here feeling comfortable talking to you. I shouldn't…"

He cut her off. "Why shouldn't you? Don't you deserve to have a friend?"

She chuckled. "I think you might want to be more than my friend."

"Someday, maybe. But see, I won't know that until I get to know you. I mean, what if you chew with your mouth open, or you never flush the toilet? I'm not sure I could be intimate with someone who does stuff like that."

She busted out laughing. "I can assure you I don't do those things."

"See, I'm willing to find out. Laney, take a chance and be my friend. Let me be your friend."

"Can I think about it?"

"I'm not going anywhere."

"All right, then, I'm going to go."

"I'm here. I've taken a few weeks off, so whenever you want to talk, I'm here. You won't be interrupting me. Although I do run in the mornings, and then go to the gym for a few hours, but I'll keep my phone with me. You know, just in case."

"Thank you, Karl."

"You are more than welcome, Laney."

Neither of them said goodbye, and neither of them hung up the phone. "Goodbye," she finally whispered.

"Goodbye."

Laney sat on the chaise lounge, looking at the end of the earth, at the huge expanse of water in front of her. She was confused and curious about this man. He was gorgeous, and she didn't understand what he wanted with her. She knew she was older than him, and she certainly wasn't a bodybuilder. Chuckling, she shook her head. "Nope, not a body-builder." She was just the opposite. Soft. Her body went to shit years ago, but she had done a hell of a job losing all the weight she'd put on. Exercise wasn't something she wanted to do. In fact, she hated it. Going to the gym, looking the way she did, with all those hard bodies, those women looking at her, and the men laughing at her, just wasn't fun nor interesting.

But this man seemed to want to get to know her, not her body. Maybe he did want to be friends, but do men really want to be just friends? Can a man and a woman just be friends? Thinking back through her life, she couldn't pull up any real friendships between men and women. Usually, it was the husband or wife of a friend, but did that even count? She didn't talk on the phone or go out to lunch with any of her friends' husbands. It was unheard of, and jealousy played a huge part in the don't factor. Did he have a girlfriend? A wife? A significant other? How would you even explain that to someone? Jealousy is such a huge emotion. It's something she couldn't remember feeling. Now, resentment and anger, those were emotions she knew well. She had such a wonderful life, and then, one day, it ended. One summer morning, it just ended. Everything spun out of control like a horror movie playing out in slow motion.

But she had promised herself she wasn't going down that rabbit hole again. That place held nothing but darkness and gloom. She had a book to finish editing and peace to find. It would be her birthday in two days, and then she was going home. She had to get ready for New York, and then she was off to Maine for Lobsterfest. She had kept the tradition. Even though it killed her to go alone, it was one of the best times, just like being at the beach. They were two things she'd promised her she would keep, no matter what.

Looking at her phone, she couldn't help but wonder how true Karl had been with his words. Was he for real? It really didn't matter if he intended to get her in bed because that wasn't something she was going to do. Disappointment was something she swore she would never allow in her world again. As long as she didn't get close to anyone, she couldn't be disappointed.

Closing her eyes, she found herself remembering his eyes and his lips. "What man on the planet has lips like that?" They were full and soft, and she could just imagine how well they felt when kissing. Looking at him, she knew he had plenty of practice. He was probably a fantastic lover and skilled. She busted out laughing. "Not that I will ever find out." But the thought still excited her, even if that was a recipe for disaster.

Before she realized what she was doing, she had her phone in her hand, looking at Google maps. He said he was in Miami. She typed it in, finding he was just over four hours away. He had said he took a few weeks off. Should she invite him to join her for the week? She was going home after this week, and she was sure the small town in Mississippi where she ended up was not someplace he would find her. Could she make a friend who was a man, or would she find herself torn between friends and one-time lovers? "Only one way to find out," she said to the phone. Pulling up his number, she pushed the message icon.

~I'm in Florida. ~

She waited to see what he would think of that.

~Funny thing. I'm in Florida as well. ~

~Would you consider a drive to maybe have dinner with me? I think I might want to try this friendship thing. Only friends, nothing more. I'm here for the rest of the week. Leaving to go home on Sunday morning. ~

~I would love to. But I must remind you that I am not going to sleep with you. ~

Laney busted out laughing.

~Good to know. I'm in Clearwater Beach. Call me when you get here. ~

~On my way. ~

Laney set her phone down, her hands shaking. What the hell was she doing? Why was she doing this? She knew why; she needed a friend. She needed to not feel alone. Seeing Don brought up a slew of memories, and she didn't want them in her mind anymore. Filling it with new memories and new experiences was what she needed. Taking a deep breath, she went inside the apartment and lay down.

Karl's heart nearly stopped when she invited him to dinner. She was four hours away, so he packed a bag then called the gym, telling Tom he would be gone for the week and would see him next Monday. He had every intention of spending the week with her. Then, out the door, he went. He had never dated anyone in Clearwater, so he wasn't worried about seeing any of the women he knew there. He didn't care either way. He was going to come clean with her. He needed to be honest. She was someone he wanted to be honest with, not someone who he gave total anonymity to. None of those women knew a fucking thing about him, about who he really was. To them, he was a gorgeous date with a rock-hard body and the skills to make them scream in bed. That's all they cared about. Shallow. All of them were that shallow. But, then again, that was his American dream. Smiling as he drove out of the city, he believed his American dream had changed. This woman had something he needed, wanted in his life, and he was prepared to drop everything to figure out what.

The miles burned under his tires as he sped down the interstate. He wasn't sure if he was excited or terrified. He knew he had to tell her about his side job. He was hopeful that she would understand. In all honesty, he knew she wouldn't; what woman would? But he was confident that since he was no longer a paid escort, she would at least appreciate that.

Finally, he reached the bridge. This place was always so busy; he wasn't sure if he could even get a hotel room, but he headed to the Hilton. Lucky for him, they had a room. He booked it for the week.

After he got settled, he pulled his phone out to text her. If she was as nervous as he was, maybe this was the easier mode of talking for now.

~On the island. Shall we meet at the beach? ~

~Well, seeing as how I asked you to dinner, I suppose we could meet at a restaurant. ~

~Your date. Tell me where. ~

She sent him the directions, and the fact it was on the fifteenth floor threw him for a loop. But he went anyway. When he got to the gate, the man at the booth asked him who he was there to see.

"Laney." Then he chuckled. "I honestly don't know her last name."

The man chuckled. "Would you be Karl with a K?"

That made him laugh. "I am."

"Can I see your license, please?"

Karl pulled out his license and handed it to the man. He watched as he wrote down his name. Handing it back to him, he said, "Thank you, Mr. Hagger. Miss Melvin is in fifteen-twenty-two. You can park in the lot for owners, in the spot marked fifteen-twenty-two-B. Have a lovely evening."

Karl smiled all the way to her door. He couldn't ever remember feeling this nervous, not even on his first paid date. He knew deep inside that this woman meant something to him, but he didn't know what; that's why he was here. His hand raised, knocking gently. He could hear soft music playing, and then the door opened, and he lost his breath. She was wearing a long dress with slits up both sides, black stockings, black slippers on her feet, and her hair was wild, thick, and full.

"You came." She smiled.

"You invited me."

She laughed. "I did. I just didn't think you would drive for four hours to have dinner with a complete stranger."

This made him laugh. "I've traveled farther to have dinner with a stranger." He didn't mean for that to slip out. The look on her face changed.

"Don't know what that means. But as long as you're here, come on in. You wouldn't mind taking your shoes off, would you?" She moved out of the way so he could come in. Closing the door, she walked past him, and he caught her scent, something he didn't catch at the event. Either that or he didn't notice, but now he noticed. He believed he was going to notice a great deal about this woman tonight. As he toed off his shoes, he looked up. Her hair hung down to her waist, and fuck if it didn't look soft and beautiful.

He followed her into the kitchen. "Do you need any help?"

She laughed. "Random fact about me: I'm not a very good cook. I mean, to me, it's edible, but I wouldn't wish that on anyone. This is carry-out. I've just been keeping it warm in the oven. I didn't know what you like to drink, so I got a bottle of red, a bottle of white, some scotch, and a bottle of whiskey. So, can I get you something to drink? I thought we could go sit on the balcony for a bit before we eat."

"I'll have whatever you are having."

"I don't drink anymore, so I'm having water."

He stood there looking at her. "Can I ask why?"

"Very long story. If I did drink, which I don't, I'd drink tequila."

He saw the bottle on the counter. Picking it up, he smiled at her. "You must have at least thought about it."

Watching the slight blush creep up her face, she said softly, "After I invited you here, I'll admit I thought I might need a bit of extra courage. This isn't something I've ever done before. Hell, it took me nine months before I let my husband meet my daughter. I will tell you this; I'm terrified right now."

He stepped closer to her. "No more than I am." Slowly, he moved his arm around her waist. "I've never been this nervous about a date in my life. Laney, don't be afraid of me."

She put her hand gently on his arm. "I'm not afraid of you. I'm afraid that you are going to want more from me, and I'm not willing to give that to you."

Leaning in, he kissed her on the forehead. "I'm not willing to take anything more than you want to give me. We are just getting to know one another. I already told you," he ducked his head down so he could look into her eyes, "I'm not going to sleep with you."

She smiled at him. Her gaze shifted to his lips as she lifted her hand from his arm and gently brushed her fingers over his lips. She quickly pulled her hand back, looking back into his eyes, and stepped back from him.

His body was filling with some kind of emotion he wasn't sure of. Her touch had been so soft. He picked up the bottle of tequila. "I'll have this if you'll have a drink with me."

Without saying a word, she turned, pulling two glasses out of the cabinet and adding ice to both of them. Then she took the bottle from him, pouring some in each glass before handing one to him.

"To new friends," she said.

"To new friends." He took a sip, but she emptied her glass in one drink, then poured some more and walked out of the room. He followed her to the balcony, where she sat on a chaise lounge, and he sat next to her.

"As a new friend, I need to tell you something. I need to be honest here, which is something I haven't completely been with anyone the majority of my adult life."

"Sounds pretty serious."

"Well, it could be, but it is what it is. I was a date for hire. That's what I was doing in Orlando."

She sat there looking at him. "You're a prostitute?"

He chuckled, not hearing disdain or disgust in her voice. "No, not a prostitute. A paid date. Sex was never paid for. It was just something that happened if both parties felt it. Never once did I take money for sex, nor would I ever, and I didn't always have sex with my dates."

"So, you were on a date when we saw each other in the restaurant?"

"No. The date took place the night before."

"Did you have sex with her?"

He looked at her, seeing only curiosity in her eyes. "Yes, I did."

"What's that like, having sex with complete strangers?"

"Over the years, it's been interesting."

"Years? How many years are we talking about?"

"Seven."

"Wow. You are a book waiting to be written."

He laughed. "You're not going to write a book about this, are you?"

She giggled, draining her glass. "I don't write books like that."

He let out a breath. "Good, because my mother is a huge fan. My dad just got her your new book."

She tilted her head. "You told your mother about me?"

Turning, so he was sitting sideways facing her, he could see the top of her lace stockings. Closing his eyes to gain some control over himself, he said, "I'm confused by the way I feel pulled toward you. This has never happened to me before. I'm nervous as hell and terrified I'm going to do something to fuck this up. But I have to try. I have to be here, and I am doing the best I can. I don't want to regret anything about this. I've never cared before what a woman had to say. Most, well, all of the women I've been with are shallow, empty, and vain. None of them care about anything but the way they look. As many of them as I have been with, not once, not one of them ever gave a shit about me or what I wanted. It wasn't what I was hired for. I was hired to accompany them, to treat them like a queen. In the end, they thought there was something more to be had, and they came on to me. They would seduce me. I am a man, after all. A pig. A slut. Who wouldn't want it? But it was all fake. They had no heart. I quit today, something I never thought I would do.

"I never wanted children, not after the shit I've seen during my service. I had a vasectomy twenty years ago. But now, after meeting you, after feeling whatever this is that I am feeling, I can't even imagine trying to do it again."

She sat there looking at him. He nearly had a heart attack when she got up and walked away. He wanted to follow her, but he knew he had just laid a huge amount of shit on her, probably something he shouldn't have done. But he needed to get it out there. He didn't want to go into this with that hanging over his head. He gave her a few minutes and then got up and went inside. He could see her standing with her hands on the counter, the bottle of tequila sitting in front of her. He moved to stand behind her, placing his glass on the counter next to hers.

"You all right?" he asked softly.

"Yes." Her words were barely audible.

Leaning down, he whispered, "Laney."

She straightened, her body coming in full contact with his chest. He froze, wanting to wrap his arms around her, but he wasn't going to do that. He promised himself he wouldn't do this. Not with her. Not yet. No fucking way was she going to become a one-night stand or a weekend fling. He was sure he wanted so much more with her. He wanted a friendship with her, something stable and lasting.

"Are you hungry?" she asked.

"I am. Do you want me to set the table?" He glanced at the table, finding it was already set. He chuckled. "How about I help you get the food out?"

She nodded. Putting the tequila away, she moved around him and opened the fridge. After getting a glass of water, she chugged it down.

Laney wasn't sure how to process what he said, so she just got up before she said something stupid. She had to commend him on his honesty. He didn't have to tell her any of that. She wasn't sure how she was feeling, but she didn't like it, so she just walked away.

Standing at the counter, she grabbed the bottle, wanting another drink, wanting to not feel anything. But when she walked out and left that life behind her, she quit drinking. Now, here she was, craving the smooth feel of the alcohol going down her throat. Getting drunk was not what she wanted or needed.

She saw him come in then felt him behind her. When he bent down and whispered in her ear, every hair on her body stood up. Closing her eyes, she straightened, her back and ass coming in full contact with his chest. He was firm, so very firm. But he didn't touch her. He didn't move either. She wasn't sure if she was happy or disappointed.

Why would he want to touch her? She'd squeezed her saggy body into a pair of Spanx and a corset. Everything about her was fake. She was just like those women he'd been with. The tequila was starting to affect her. Moving around him, she grabbed a glass and filled it with water from the fridge. It was cool and soothing as the cold liquid slid down her throat. It was ridiculous for her to feel like this, to want this man, and to want this man to want her. She wasn't worthy, far from it. She was almost embarrassed at her body. If only it were ten years ago, this might have worked. But not now. There was no way.

She turned around after setting her empty glass on the counter. Not expecting it, she turned into his chest. His hand slid up to rest on her hip. Slowly lifting her head, she saw him looking at her with those piercing blue eyes.

"Whatever is running through your head right now, put it away." His words were soft and sincere.

"You just don't understand."

"Maybe not. But I will. One day." His other hand came up, and his thumb brushed along her bottom lip. "One day, I will."

She wanted to kiss him. God did she want to kiss him. But she couldn't. She just stood there, frozen to the floor while they looked into each other's eyes. He stopped touching her and slowly withdrew his hand before stepping back, so she didn't feel so crowded.

"We should eat. I think the tequila is getting to me. I feel a bit flushed."

He chuckled. "Let's do this then. Tell me what you need."

Laughing, she said, "Yeah, that's probably not a good idea. But grab some pot-holders and let's do this."

She handed him all the containers, and one by one, he put them on the table. When they finished, she grabbed the two bottles of wine and the opener, and they sat down. They ate and talked about nothing and everything. She discovered that he owned a gym in Miami. He'd made enough money as an escort to move his parents here from Denmark. She discovered that he was Danish, even though his accent wasn't that noticeable anymore. Certain words, she could hear it, but other than that, she would have never known.

She discovered that he had an older brother, two younger brothers, and two younger sisters. She told him about her family, that she had two sisters and a brother but was only ever close with one of them.

When they finished, he helped her clean up, and then they got comfortable on the couch. "You are an exceptional writer," he complimented her.

"Thank you."

"What made you want to write?"

She sat there looking at him, not sure she could get the words out without completely breaking down. Her reasons were no more, and this was not the time nor the place to tell him. "I can't answer that right now."

"Fair enough. I'm in no hurry."

"Thank you and thank you for coming all this way for just dinner."

He laughed. "I didn't just come for dinner. I'm staying at the Hilton. I'll be here all week. I told you, I want to get to know you. When you leave, I'll leave. So, I heard you say that you would see your friends in New York."

She nodded. "There is this big book event there next month. My publisher thinks I should go. I've been out of the circuit for a while now, and she thinks my fans need to see me. Then, after that, I'm heading up to Maine."

"What's in Maine?"

She giggled as she stood. "Lobsterfest. We've been going for the past ten years. So I thought I would…" She stopped talking, turning away from him, her eyes glassing over. "I love lobster," she finished, "so I go every year."

"I've never been to Maine. Been to New York a few times. Not sure I like that city."

"I hate it, but the event is in a hotel, so I don't really need to go anywhere. It's the only event I fly to. My publisher has a car pick me up at the airport and drop me off after the event, where I usually grab a rental and head up to Maine every year. Last year, I drove all the way there by myself. I didn't do the event." She wiped her tears. Holding this in was harder than she thought, but they had shared enough deep stuff for the evening. She felt him stand and move behind her.

"Should I go?"

She felt her body move just a little until his chest was at her back. "I don't know."

"Laney." His voice was deep.

He wrapped his arm around her waist and stepped into her. She rested her hand on his, their fingers entwining at her waist. "I'm not going to cross this line with you. I want so much more. But if you need me to stay for a while, I am more than willing."

Her heart jumped when he mentioned crossing the line. "What line, Karl? What line do you want to cross?"

"No line, Laney. I was truthful when I said I wanted... no, needed to get to know you. Somehow, I don't think we've touched the surface of who we are."

"No, I suppose we haven't." She turned in his embrace, her hands resting on his arms. She could feel his muscles and found it weird that she didn't feel them the night they danced. Maybe because she wasn't aware of how she was changing. Tilting her head up, she saw him looking at her. When he licked his lips, she was sure he was going to kiss her, but he didn't move. Neither of them moved. "I'll be on the beach tomorrow if you want to join me."

"I would like that very much. Random fact about me: I am trying with all that I am not to do this." She felt his fingers move down to her thigh. "I so very much want to see these." He gently brushed the top of her thigh where the lace to her stockings was, then moved his hand away.

She smirked at him. "Random fact about me: I didn't wear them for you. I wore them for me. Pretty things make me feel good."

His smile lit up the room. "They make me feel good, as well. They've been driving me crazy all night. This, as well." His hand slid from her waist, up along the laces on the back of her corset.

She smiled at him. "Does the fact that I am wearing this make you uncomfortable? Do you think I want you to slip my dress off so you can look at me?"

He shook his head slowly. "Not uncomfortable. Not in a million years. But yes, I would love to look at you. But not tonight. Not tomorrow night or the night after that. I am a very patient man, and if I never see you in that manner, I'm all right with that as well. I'm not here to get you into bed. I'm here because this is the place I want to be."

"You say all the right things, Karl with a K." Her voice was soft and breathy. "All the right words."

"That may be true, but I don't think I've ever meant them like I do at this moment."

She smiled at him, stepping back. "I'm an early riser. I hate to waste the day." She moved into the kitchen. "I've wasted so many of them." She poured a glass of water. "Oh, random fact about me: I'm allergic to chlorine."

He smiled at her. "Good to know. So, no pools?"

"Nope, and no tap water."

"How do you shower?"

"I have special filters on my pipes at home that filter it out of the water, and since I rent this place every year, the owner let me put them on his pipes, so the water here is pure."

"Well, on the off chance that you might come to my house one day, where would I find these special water filters?"

She busted out laughing. "A little ahead of yourself, aren't you?"

He moved right into her space, right up to her face. If either of them moved, their mouths would have touched. In a deep whisper, he said, "Hopeful. I am hopeful that one day you will come to my house." He seared his lust for her into her soul. Stepping back, he said, "You'd like it there. It's on the beach. Fifteenth floor, because you can see the water without all the noise. Same reason I'm guessing that you are in this apartment."

She stood there looking at him. Mesmerized by him. Setting her glass down, she stepped forward. "Who are you, Karl with a K?"

His hand came up to touch her cheek. "A man who is smitten, I think. A man who is amazed that a woman like you would even entertain the thought of me after what I told you concerning the life I've been leading."

"I'm not anyone special."

He chuckled. "I'll put money on the fact that you are. Now, I will see you on the beach at nine. Thank you for dinner and your time. But tomorrow, and in the foreseeable future, it's on me. I am a gentleman, but I'm also a man and insist on taking the lead."

She giggled. "So sure of yourself, aren't you?"

He turned and moved to the door, putting his shoes on. "I am." He smiled. "Goodnight, Laney."

"Goodnight, Karl."

He opened the door and walked out. He didn't get far before he bent over, putting his hands on his knees. He was actually dizzy. "Jesus." He had to get out of there. He was going to kiss her, and that's not what she wanted. He had no clue what was happening to him. When he walked out of the elevator, he dialed his mom.

"Sweetheart, is everything all right? It's late. You never call this late."

"Everything is fine, Mom. I just need some advice."

She laughed. "Is it Mel?"

He chuckled. "Yeah, Mom, it's Mel. I just had dinner with her. Something is happening to me, and I'm not sure I know what, or what to do it about."

"Tell me, sweetheart."

"Mom, she's incredible. I want to be the asshole guy who takes advantage of her, but my inner self keeps telling me to stop."

"Oh, honey, keep stopping. She has been through a great deal. I can't imagine what she has been through, but from what I heard on that Facebook, she just walked away from the world. To do that, she must have been suffering a great deal. The death of a child is something I don't think I would survive. Sweetheart, you just aren't supposed to out-live your children."

"Mom, she hasn't told me any of this. I can't say anything to her about it."

"Karl, it was all over the news. She is a famous writer. You would have to be dead to have not heard about it."

He chuckled. Dead or self-absorbed. Such a selfish life he has led. "Mom, I'm struggling to maintain my self-control."

"Really? Karl, I didn't think you enjoyed the company of a woman of her stature."

He busted out laughing. His mother mentioning stature was her being polite about a woman's looks. "Mom, you are the one who taught me that it's not about what a person looks like, but what's inside that counts."

She laughed. "I know, sweetheart, but every woman I've ever seen you with on your fancy dates was thin and beautiful."

"Well, you won't be seeing that anymore. It's what's inside this woman that's making me re-think my life. I feel like she is a magnet, pulling me into her orbit. I'm so far out of my league here, and I need your help."

"Sweetheart just be the kind man I raised. Let your heart feel. You've kept it closed off far too long. What happened when you were young was a very long time ago. She never would have stayed with you. She was one of those shallow girls. No heart, no feeling for anything but herself. From what Ester told me, she is a single mother of four children, each with a different father. Be glad she dumped you."

Her words hurt. Karl still felt the sting of her burn. Thirty years ago, he felt love like that, or what he perceived love to be. She was the reason he joined the service. But if he thought about it, it was the best thing that could have ever happened to him.

"You're right, Mom. Thanks. I love you."

"I love you, too. Sweetheart, be careful with her."

"I will. Goodnight.

"Goodnight."

He started his car and headed to the hotel. Once in his room, he dropped his clothes and crawled into bed. He was so confused. Not about what he wanted, but with how to control himself. He felt for this woman like no other woman in his life. Closing his eyes, he went to sleep. His phone vibrated on the table, waking him up. He walked over and picked it up. It was three in the morning. He smiled when he saw it was a message from her.

~I can't sleep. I can't stop thinking. ~

"Me neither, beautiful. Me neither."

~Want to talk about it? ~

~You're up. ~

~I am now. ~

~I'm sorry. Go back to sleep. ~

"No way that's going to happen." He dialed her number.

"Hi."

"Hi, what's wrong?"

"I, um… I…"

"Laney. I think I know."

"Karl, why didn't you kiss me?"

"Because you're not ready for me to kiss you. I'm not ready to kiss you. I'm afraid if I kiss you that I won't want to stop."

She giggled a soft giggle. "Well, thank you for saying that. I think I can sleep now. I'm sorry for waking you with this stupid stuff. I'm really not this insecure."

"Random fact about me: neither am I. I'm pretty confident, but you make me nervous. Very nervous."

"Yeah?"

"Oh yeah. Goodnight, Laney."

"Goodnight, Karl."

He hung up the phone with a smile on his face and went back to bed.

CHAPTER EIGHT

When her alarm clock went off, she rolled over, looking out the window at the end of the world. She needed to get in the shower and get down to the beach.

She was sitting in the sand when he walked up. "Good morning, Laney." He sat down next to her.

"After last night and my crazy middle of the night hysterics, I wasn't sure you were going to show up."

He chuckled. "I'm afraid it would take a great deal more than that to keep me away."

"I did a lot of thinking about the things you told me. About being a paid escort. I guess I shouldn't be shocked by it. I mean, look at you."

"I look at me every morning in the mirror. I don't feel like I'm anything special. I feel cheated and cheap. I was fine with that life. I knew I never wanted to have children, and I never really met anyone worth giving it all up. The women are beautiful, but they're so self-involved. So fake, and well, I didn't see myself spending my life with someone I couldn't have a conversation with."

"Karl, I'm self-involved. I'm not worth you giving up your life. Trust me."

"I didn't give up my life because I met you. I gave it up because it demeans the man I am. None of those women ever bothered to talk to me. They just wanted someone who would complement them, satisfy them in bed. Without sounding harsh, they were just horny women who wanted a no-attachment fling."

"And you were the guy to give it to them."

"Not always, but yes. I'm not the only guy who works there. Some of these women had been with all of the guys."

"That's sad, to think that they didn't think more of themselves." She looked at him and smiled. "I guess, good for you. All that sex was probably too hard to pass up."

"If I'm honest, at first, it was great. But the more time that passed, it became routine. Keep in mind, I didn't have sex with all of them." He laughed. "Not even as many as you might think."

"Oh, you don't want to know what I think."

He leaned into her. "I want to know everything you think."

"So, did you really quit?"

"Yeah, it was time."

"And it wasn't because of me? Because I'm not sure where this is going, but I'm pretty sure it isn't that place at all."

"You challenge me to be a better person, to be the person, the man my mother raised. If she knew I was doing that, I'm pretty sure she'd kill me. I know my father would disown me. It was a way to make good money fast."

"And get all that free sex."

"Exactly." He laughed. "But it was just sex. All they wanted was for me to fuck them stupid. Sorry for being so blunt."

She was laughing. "Oh my God. Can someone really be fucked stupid?" She had tears rolling down her cheeks from laughing.

He started laughing with her. "It's not hard when they are already stupid." That sent them both into an even heavier laugh. When they calmed down, he smiled at her. "Did you have breakfast yet?"

Wiping her face, she shook her head. "No, I thought I'd wait for you. There's a nice place up the beach. We can walk."

≈

He helped her up, watching her dust the sand off her dress. She was wearing a cute dress that flowed nearly to the ground. They walked down the beach together, and he couldn't help but wonder if she was wearing the corset again. When they walked up to the door, he casually put his hand on her back as he opened the door for her. *Yep, she's wearing it again.*

When they finished breakfast, they just walked around, talking and sharing things about themselves. His curiosity was piqued about what she'd said the night he met her. They were sitting on a bench, enjoying an ice cream.

"Can I ask you something personal?"

He felt her body tense up. "As long as you respect me enough to accept that I might not be able to answer it, yes."

"Okay. But why wouldn't you be able to answer it?"

She smiled. "Is that your question?" He shook his head. "There are some things I'm not willing to talk about. Some things I can't talk about. Some things…" She looked at him. "What's your question?"

He smiled. "Well, that first night in the café, you said something, and it's been rolling around in my head."

She started to giggle. "You want to know why I've been responsible for my own orgasms?"

He laughed. "Yeah, I would. I mean, wouldn't you if I had said that?"

"Probably. Let's see. Well, geez, that's hard to explain without all the boring life shit in between. Maybe if this friendship thing goes well, I might be inclined to tell you all of the boring details." She smiled. "Short story, my husband wasn't a good lover. In fact, he sucked in bed. Small dick, and I think he might be gay. When we would have sex, it lasted less than five minutes, and it was all about him getting off and not me. So, I would take care of myself."

"I'm so sorry."

"Oh, no. It was normal. I knew I'd made the biggest mistake of my life the first New Year's Eve after we were married. But he had already formed a great bond with my… Well, he was a nice man, a good man, a kind man. Very smart, and I think that's what was so attractive about him."

"What happened on New Year's Eve?"

"I'd planned this romantic evening. I even bought some sexy lingerie. We were in our family room. I'd made up the floor, had a carpet picnic. We were doing good until we started to kiss. Then he just got up and said, 'I can't do this. I feel like I'm being forced to perform.'"

"Fuck."

"I know. I knew it then, but I stayed. There were plenty more instances over the years. He is a very self-absorbed person. Most of the time, I would just smile and ignore his comments. If the conversation strayed away from what he was talking about, he would make me feel like shit." She chuckled.

"Can I ask why you stayed?"

"I didn't. I left."

"Laney, how long were you married to him?"

"Before I left?" He nodded. "Just about fifteen years."

When he pulled her to his chest and hugged her, she felt something stir inside of her. He kissed her on the head. "I'm so sorry."

Pulling away, she smiled. "Thank you, but I stayed for other reasons. It was safe."

"Come on." He took her hand, entwining their fingers. She looked down at his hand. He smiled at her. "Don't overanalyze. Let's go have some fun."

The way she felt when he took her hand was not what she expected. Last night, when he touched her thigh and made the innuendo, she felt her panties get wet. This man was dangerous for her. If she let him, he was going to hurt her. Was this what she wanted? Maybe not, but how could she resist the attention of probably the best-looking man she'd ever seen? His lips alone were to die for. She let him pull her along until they ended up in a game room. He raised his eyebrows at her. "Now, this is the place to have some fun."

Laney decided to just go with it. She needed some fun, and fun they had. At the end of their two hours in the game room, they had thousands of tickets. She got a small stuffed unicorn as her prize. Laughing, she put it in her bag, and they went to have lunch.

"You look like you're getting a bit of sun. Maybe we should head in for a while."

"I'm game. It is a bit warm out here." She wanted to take her corset off. They walked hand in hand back to her apartment. "Are you going to make a habit of this?" She held up their hands.

He smiled at her. "Yep."

When they got inside, she excused herself, heading to the bedroom. She shut the door and went to the bathroom. Peeling off her clothes, she jumped in the shower to relieve some of the heat. Walking out into the living room in one of her summer shirts and skirt, she found him with his eyes closed on the couch. She stood there looking at him. He was so beautiful.

"I'm not sleeping," he said softly, opening his eyes.

"What was it like, being used like that?"

"I'm a guy. It was free sex. I got off."

She smiled. "But did any of them ever get you off? Touch you, take care of you?"

He looked at her. "It's not supposed to be like that. A woman's pleasure is all that matters."

She shook her head. "In my experience, that's not true."

She watched him stand and move toward her. She stepped back. His hand came up and touched her face. "Your experience has not been a good one. You were just with the wrong man."

"Like you were with the wrong women," she countered.

"Real men don't just take. They make sure the woman is satisfied before they get off."

"Is that what you do? Make sure they are satisfied?"

"It's what I did. Not what I do."

"Karl?"

"Yeah."

"Are you…"

"No, I'm not. I don't want that from you, and you certainly don't want it from me. Not when everything you know about me is fresh in your mind. I would never want you to feel as if I was using you, because I never will, and I don't want to feel like I'm giving you the one thing you've never had."

She licked her lips. "Thank you."

"Never thank me for treating you like you deserve to be treated."

She moved away from him. She had to, or she was going to kiss him. "Did you want something to drink? I have cold tea and lemonade."

"Lemonade sounds great. Why don't you tell me about these books you write?"

She laughed. "Well, they aren't like most."

"I loved the one you gave me. Are they all like that?"

"What do you mean, like that?" She handed him his glass and moved to the couch.

Karl followed her, sitting down by her. "Well, it was a romance book, but isn't there supposed to be sex in them?"

She spit her lemonade out all over the place, laughing. "Romance isn't always about sex. It's about the connection between two people, between their souls, if you would. Something I guess I've never had. You know, those who can't, teach."

"So, you've never had a kiss like the one in your book?"

"No. Have you?"

"No, but I'd like to think that one day I will."

"Make sure when you find her that she's the one. Make sure she feels it to the bottom of her toes. I think we, as women, want that at least one time in our lives."

"I'll keep that in mind."

They sat and talked for a bit. Her eyes drooped lower and lower.

"You're tired."

"I am."

She watched him get up and put his glass on the counter. "Will you have dinner with me tonight?"

She got up and followed him. "I'd like that, but I don't want to go out. Maybe we could just get Chinese or something."

"You got it. I'll be back around seven." Leaning in, he kissed her on the forehead.

She watched him walk out the door, then headed to the couch.

Karl made his way back to his hotel to shower and relax. What he really wanted to do was curl up on her couch with her. He kept playing the day over and over. The conversations. He couldn't believe she had never experienced a kiss like the ones she wrote about. Reaching for her book, he opened it to the bookmarked page and read her words.

She went to walk away in a fit of anger, and he reached out and grabbed her arm. When she turned, he wrapped his hand in her hair, fisting it close to her head. Their eyes locked as he moved her against the wall, placing his legs on either side of her. Tilting her head up to meet his, he kissed her, putting everything he had into it. He was touching her soul, marking her heart, making her forever his.

He wiped at his eyes. She had never been kissed like that. She dreamed of it. She desired it, but she'd never experienced it. It made him sad. He didn't feel sorry for her; he felt sad that she had never had that experience in life.

Closing the book, he lay down and closed his eyes with her on his mind. He was so afraid of how he was feeling, scared he would scare her away, make her run from him, and he didn't want that. He wanted her to stay, and he wanted to stay with her. There was nothing he could do but spend time with her and make her see that she was worthy of such feelings like she wrote. He was enjoying himself, something he'd never done before. Something he was sure he'd never wanted. Spending all of his time with one woman made him skittish;

maybe it was because he was always with the wrong kind of woman. Was she the wrong kind of woman? He didn't believe that, not for a minute. He was so glad he stayed that night. He planned on leaving like he did every time he chose to sleep with one of them. He would do his thing and then leave when they fell asleep. He hated the awkward morning after with them, maybe because he didn't really like them. He used their bodies for his release. He gave as much of himself as he was willing to give. After what happened when he was younger, he never gave his heart away again. He never wanted to give it away again. But those were childish memories, childish feelings. He wasn't in love. Hell, he wasn't even sure what love was, for that matter.

What he knew now was that he wanted to see her. He wanted to be with her, listening to her talk, sharing their stories and thoughts. She listened attentively and responded as if she was really interested in getting to know him, and that made him feel good. Special. He had never felt that. Even when she was smart mouthing him, he couldn't stop his smile. He couldn't hide what he was feeling.

Looking at the clock, he wanted it to be six, not four. He wanted to get Chinese food and go back and spend more time with her. But he couldn't shake this feeling that when she left, he wouldn't see her again. Grabbing his phone, he looked up this book event in New York. He called the hotel, booked a room, and asked how he could get tickets to all the events. The girl on the other end assured him that she would have everything ready for him when he checked in. If she was leaving, then he was following. Was he a stalker? No, he didn't think so. But she was famous. People knew who she was. Well, they knew what she wanted them to know. No one knew her real name. He decided to send her a message.

~I don't want to be here. ~

He wasn't expecting her to answer him. He knew she was tired. She'd been falling asleep while he was there. But his phone dinged.

~I'm sorry. Are you going home then? ~

"Oh, God, no."

~I meant here in this room. Not here with you. ~

~Karl, what are we doing? ~

He dialed her number.

"Hi," she answered.

"Hi. I thought we were becoming friends."

"That wasn't a friend text. That was something more. I'm not sure this is a good idea."

His heart sped up as he started to panic. "It's a good idea, Laney. You're just scared like I am."

"Get some food and come over. I think we need to talk."

"You sure?"

"Yes. Goodbye, Karl."

He smiled and hung up. When he got to her place, she was waiting for him. She didn't say much as they ate. After they cleaned everything up, he watched her pour tequila in two glasses before she drank one of them down. Karl knew what she was going to do; he could feel it. There's no way he was going to let her walk away. She poured more into her empty glass and walked into the living room, handing him the other. She sat in the chair across from him.

"I had so much fun today." She shook her head. "My life isn't about having fun. I'm too old for that. I need to use what time I have left living with the choices I've made. You, Karl, are not one of those choices." Her eyes on him were thoughtful, serious. "I'm sure I'm much older than you, and I just don't understand what you want from me because I am not going to sleep with you. I made some stupid mistakes in my life. I've done things I'm not proud of, but I had my reasons, and now all my reasons are gone, so it's just me. I need to make the best of what I have left." He watched as she emptied her glass again before setting it on the table. He wanted to say something, but he wasn't sure if she was done. With her eyes never leaving his, she sat there looking at him. "You are far too beautiful to be wasting your time with me. Honestly, I'm nothing. Not anymore, not since…" She stopped, and he watched her internal struggle in her eyes. When she looked away, she picked up the glass and walked back into the kitchen. He heard the glass hit the counter. Fighting with himself not to go in there and grab her up in his arms, he waited for her to come back in. When she did, she had another full glass in her hand. "I can't do this with you. I don't want to do this with you. The more time we spend together, the harder this will be when I leave."

"For who, you?" he asked quietly.

She stared at him for what felt like an hour. She smiled. "So sure of yourself."

He smiled a small smile. "Not anymore. Random fact about me: I don't do anything halfway."

"There isn't anything to do all the way with me."

"You are making that decision for me, not giving me the opportunity to discover things on my own. You are controlling, or trying to control what is happening here, and I don't think you can. Laney, even if you walk away and never look back, that still isn't going to stop this. I can see it in your eyes; you're scared, and that's where this is coming from. I'm scared, too. I'm terrified that when I walk out that door, I am never going to see you again, and I am just getting to know you. You want to know why I did what I did? Because I have been afraid my entire life of getting my heart ripped out, so I made this persona up that couldn't get attached to anyone."

"So what, you're attached to me? You don't even know me."

"No, but I want to. I want to know your favorite thing to do. I want to know your favorite food, your favorite color. I want to know what makes you write such beautiful stories. I want to know how you take your coffee in the morning. I want to know what kind of tea you drink that turns the water red. I want to know why you wear a corset. I want to know why you believe you aren't sexy as hell. I haven't wanted these things in my life. But I want them with you."

"I can't be an option for you."

"Why? Because you made some mistakes? We all have. My life has been one mistake after another. But I got up every day, and I accepted them and moved forward. Our lives aren't things we can live in glass balls. Lives shatter every day. It's our strength that picks us up and moves us forward. Is life fragile? Yes, it is, but you can't ever be happy if you're terrified of breaking. I'm telling you that I want to be here to catch you when you think you are going to break."

He watched as the tears fell down her cheeks. "I already broke, and no one was there." He almost didn't hear her.

"Did you let anyone catch you?"

She shook her head. "Nothing could stop my fall."

"Tell me," he whispered. "Tell me, Laney. I want to know why you think you are so broken, so unredeemable that you can't allow yourself to feel."

"I feel, Karl. I feel so deeply that I can't swim. I'm drowning, and I'm not so sure I want help."

They sat there looking at one another, her tears falling slowly down her cheeks. He fought hard with himself not to get up, not to pull her into his arms. She needed him in so many other ways, and he knew she did. He knew she was feeling this pull between them, and she was fighting it hard.

"Tell me."

She moved so fast when she got up that he flinched. After swallowing the amber liquid in her glass, she moved to the kitchen. If he didn't stop her, she was going to get drunk. He was a big man, and he would definitely be feeling the effects of that much tequila.

He walked into the kitchen as she was bringing the glass to her lips. Gently, he put his hand on her arm to stop her. "Is this the wisest choice?"

"It's the only choice." She drank it all in one go.

Karl took the glass from her, setting it on the counter. "Come here." He pulled her into his arms, wrapping her in his cocoon. "I'll hold you." She wrapped her arms around his waist as she sunk into his embrace. He felt her shatter in his arms, standing in the low light of the kitchen. Her body shook as she silently cried. He hoped this was a turning point and that she would stop running. He found himself wanting to be her rock in the storm. He wanted her to need him, but somehow, deep inside, he knew she didn't, and strength like that is something he had never known. She wasn't hiding who she was; she'd told him she was damaged. He didn't care. He didn't care one bit. He kissed the top of her head. His mother had told him what happened to her, but he needed her to tell him so he could help her. So she could feel his care, and he did care more than he ever thought possible. They stood there for a long time while she cried, while he held her. His heart expanded for this woman in his arms. He knew he could never let her go. Just knowing her for the past few days felt like a lifetime, as if he had known her always.

As she calmed down, she pulled back and walked away. He watched her walk into what he believed to be the bedroom. He waited where he was, leaning on the counter. When she came out, she stood looking at him. He could see her eyes were red and swollen, and her nose was red from blowing it. She was beautiful, real. Like no one who came before her, she was perfect; at least, to him she was.

He watched her swallow. "Will you hold me?"

He stepped forward, reaching out for her hand. He was nervous. Slowly, she put hers in his and moved to the couch. He got on and lay on his side. When she crawled on and moved to lay in his arms, he held his breath. His eyes closed as she placed her head softly on his bicep. Her hand gently rested on his chest. He slowly moved his hand and placed it on her hip.

"I don't know how to do this, how to talk about it. I don't know how to tell you." Her voice was so soft.

"Wherever you want to begin, I'm sure it will be fine. As long as you begin." He whispered against her head, "I'll be right here. Tell me what you want, what you can."

She nodded and snuggled closer to him. "You smell good," she cooed.

"Thank you."

"When I used to drink, I was out with my friends and met a beautiful stranger. He paid attention to me, said all the right things. He made me feel beautiful and desired. I was stupid back then. I thought all the beautiful words meant something, but they didn't. They were just words to get me involved, to get me into bed." He understood a bit more as she spoke. "Of course, I was young, stupid, and naive. He was so beautiful, and he was so tender and loving, caring. We had a relationship for a few months, and then I got pregnant. Of course, he left. His mother didn't like me, and she didn't want me to be her daughter-in-law. So, he left me. I, of course, now totally in love with him and needy of him, tried to no avail to get him back. Even the lure of having his child was nothing compared to what his mother wanted for him."

"I'm sorry."

She shook her head. "It's the ways of men. Well, I had a daughter. Her name was Anna. She was my shining star. So precious, so beautiful, and so very smart. Our life was hard, rough. We were very poor, but it didn't matter because we had each other." He pulled her closer to him. "I had to do something to make our life better. I have this natural ability to argue with people, so I thought I might try my hand at law school. It went well. It was hard, but we did it together. Me and Anna, the dynamic duo. Needless to say, I was very protective of her. Never did a man appear in her life. I told you I've been responsible for my own orgasms, and well, she would be why."

He lay there, holding her in his arms, realizing the book she wrote was her story. Everything. "I was in my fourth year, working in the courts when I met Don. He was there testifying in some corporate cover-up. He approached me in the hallway, asked me out. I figured why not; it was just lunch. Well, lunch led to dinner, and you can guess where that led. He was charming, older, divorced, and already had children. He was a very nice man, a very safe man. It took me nine months before I allowed him to meet Anna. I needed to be sure. They became fast buddies. A few months later, he asked me to marry him, and I said yes."

He closed his eyes, taking a deep breath. She stopped talking for a few minutes. She was completely relaxed in his arms. He thought she had fallen asleep. His hand moved to secure her in his embrace, wrapping around her waist, pulling her closer until every part of their bodies touched. He felt her hand slide under his arm to his back as she shifted herself.

"That New Year's Eve I told you about, that was the day I realized I had made the biggest mistake of my life. But by then, it was too late; he had already gotten inside Anna's heart. I couldn't hurt her like that. She had come alive. She was all that mattered. So, I stopped feeling for him, and I lived my life in silence, despising the man. He tried so hard, but then he didn't. I had a law degree, and I was beneath him in every way. He didn't have a problem with showing me or telling me. Everything was about him. He would tell me all the time with his actions." Karl was shocked that she'd stayed with him, but he understood she'd done it for her daughter. "As the years went by, I focused on Anna—taught her, loved her, lived my life for her. I was kind and included him in everything to do with her. When he wanted to have sex, he would ask me so he could put it in his calendar." She chuckled but not in a funny way. "I was just another appointment for him. But it wasn't enjoyable. He would touch me just so he could get hard. He made comments about my stomach, my breasts. He told me once that he dreamed of being with a woman with a hard body while he was getting himself hard. I refused to let him take me bare. I didn't want to have his child. I didn't want him to touch me. But I needed to keep him happy. He would use my body to get off. When he finished, he would get up and leave the room. We didn't cuddle, and he never held me. Hell, he never kissed me. Well, he did once, and he spit in my mouth so I refused to kiss him like that again." She was twisting his heart with her words. He felt her sadness, her anguish. "He told me once, toward the end, that I was too loose, and he would be better satisfied if he could take me in the ass." She shook her head. Her body started to tremble, and her tears came again. "Wh-who says th-that to th-the w-woman you say y-you l-love?"

"Aww, sweetheart." He felt his tears welling in his eyes. His leg slowly wrapped around hers. "No one should ever say that. Shh, it's over now."

He held her tight while she sobbed. He held her until she fell asleep in his arms. Closing his eyes, he slept with her, holding her. He promised himself he was never going to let her feel like this again.

As she woke in his arms, wrapped in his embrace, she felt safe for the first time in her life. He was massive compared to her, something she hadn't realized until this moment. He was a thick man, muscular, and God did he smell wonderful. She moved her hand, sliding it from behind him to rest on his chest. She knew he was awake when his breathing changed. "Thank you," she whispered as he pulled back a little. Her fingers grazed his lips. They were so soft, so full. They felt like silk under her fingers. She wanted to kiss him, but it wasn't a good idea. This was all it would ever be. It was dark in the room, so she couldn't really see his blue eyes.

"You don't ever have to thank me. Are you all right?"

Pulling her hand away, she leaned into his chest. "I'm never going to be all right, or right again. She's gone, my heart is broken, and it will never be whole again."

"Tell me about her."

"She was so smart, so beautiful. I remember how excited she was all the time about science. I wanted her to be able to go to the best schools. So, I thought I would try my hand at writing."

"Aren't you a lawyer? Why didn't you do that?"

"I am. I graduated, but I never took the bar. I married Don. My first two books did all right, then somehow, a publisher got hold of one of them and approached me. The rest just happened. I made enough money to pay for her college, and then some. When it was time for her to apply to colleges, she applied to all of them." She chuckled. "I thought she was crazy, but she got into most of them. Her choice was always Dartmouth. She said she wanted them to court her, but she always knew where she was going. When she left for school, I think I fell into some sort of depression. My books became filled with even more sadness. They were selling like crazy, but I was lonely, and with that came a very unhealthy relationship with food. It was a great comfort, and I just got bigger and bigger as the years went by. I had always planned on leaving Don. I just wanted her to be happy while she went to med school. After she graduated, she was invited to do her internship at Boston Mass General, her hospital of choice.

"She was home for a few weeks before she started her internship, to pack up all of her things. It was the Monday after she got home from touring the hospital. I was in the kitchen, making coffee when I heard her bedroom door open. She called for me, and I looked around the corner. Her hands were on her head." She started to cry again. He pulled her closer, but she put her hand on his chest and sat up. Then she moved away. "When I looked into her eyes, she said, 'Mom, my head hurts.' Then she went down, slamming to the floor on her knees. I dropped my cup on the floor and made it to her before her body hit the floor. She died in my arms with tears falling down the side of her face. I can remember hearing myself scream her name as she went limp, her hands falling to the floor. My beautiful girl was gone. Everything I was, everything I thought I knew was gone. My heart broke, and I'm terrified it will never heal."

He was up and had his arms around her, holding her while she cried. Her legs buckled, and he picked her up and carried her to the bedroom. He climbed on the bed, crawled to the middle of it, and sat holding her. He was sure she had never told that story to anyone. He was sure that she had held the pain inside all this time. It all made sense to him now, the things she said to him, how damaged she was, how broken.

Her book was her story.

When Laney woke, she was alone in her bed. The sky was lighting up. It was dawn. Sitting up, she looked around the darkened room. He wasn't there. She got up and used the bathroom, brushing her teeth and washing her face. Looking at herself in the mirror, her eyes were puffy, her hair a mess. Grabbing her hairbrush, she pulled it through. Today was her birthday. "You're an old lady now," she said to her reflection. When she walked into the living room, she hoped to find him asleep on the couch, but he wasn't there. On the table was a piece of paper. She picked it up.

Thank you for sharing with me. For telling me. I didn't think it was right that I stay over, even though I had a fight with myself about leaving you. I didn't want you to feel embarrassed. Let's spend the day together and have some fun.

Karl with a K

Her smile was huge. She didn't feel embarrassed; she felt a bit lighter. She had never told anyone what happened, what it did to her to watch Anna die in her arms. She had a hard time pushing the memory away. Her focus for her own sanity were the beautiful memories of the life she had. Reaching for her necklace, her fingers found the gold heart she had given Anna when she graduated from High School. "I love you, beautiful girl. Forever," she whispered, looking up at the ceiling. The gentle knock on the door made her smile. She turned and looked at it, wondering if he would knock again or if he would come back later. Nope, not leaving. She walked over and looked out the peephole. He was standing there with something in his hands, so she opened the door. His smile warmed her in a way she was sure she didn't know.

"Good morning." He held up a tray. "I brought coffee and some junk food."

"Well, who am I to deny a gorgeous man and free junk food?"

He laughed as she moved out of his way so he could come in. "I didn't know what you like in your coffee, so I just got black."

"Black is good. I have sugar. What else do you have in that bag?" She reached for it.

He pulled it out of her reach. "Oh no, this is my surprise." She laughed, sticking her lip out in a pout. "Oh, all right." He handed her the bag. She did a cute little, happy girl dance as she moved to the counter. Reaching up, she grabbed some plates. He had bought a few donuts and croissants, so they sat and ate while drinking their coffee. After she felt a bit off, like something was going on that she wasn't aware of. She finally got the nerve to ask him, "What's wrong?"

He smiled at her. "Not a thing. Why, do I seem like there is something wrong?"

"Well, it feels a bit weird. I've never told anyone the things I told you last night." Her voice was quiet. "I feel like I… I don't know."

"Like you bared your soul to me, and then I left in the middle of the night?"

"Like I was one of your women. You wanted me to tell you, and then when it was over, you left."

He reached across and took her hand in his. "I didn't think it was right for me to sleep over. Yes, I never slept over with any of those women, so I can see how you would feel weird."

"But you stayed that night."

"I did, and it was the rightest decision I have ever made in my life. I will admit that everything you told me took me down a road I've never been down, and I wanted to absorb it and make sure I was feeling the way I am feeling. Holding you in my arms was clouding my thoughts. It took a great deal for me to walk out of that bedroom, but it was the right thing to do. Seeing as how I am on the road to doing what is right, I figured I should continue doing what is right."

"I'm still not sure this is the best thing to do. I am so much older than you. Won't your friends question you, talk about you?"

He laughed. "How old do you think I am?"

"I don't know, maybe forty."

"That's what people believe. That's what I tell them. That's how old my ex-boss thinks I am. But I'm going to be forty-eight. Is that old enough for you?"

She laughed. "Well, it's a bit older. I'm still going on the record, saying this isn't a good idea. Anna died just about three years ago, and I'm still not over it. I live twelve hours away, and I'm not moving. It took me a long time to find that town, and my house is there. I'm not even sure you would fit in my house."

"Listen to me. You are going about this in a clinical, check-list sort of way. Why don't we just let it play out? Let us learn and grow. I don't want to regret not knowing you. I'm not asking you for a sexual relationship. I'm asking you to get to know me, for you to let me get to know you. Let's become friends. I want... no, I need to have you in my life. If we never get to the bedroom, I'm all right with that. Honestly."

"Can I ask you something?"

"Anything at all. Anytime."

"While we are getting to know one another, while we are apart, are you going to be working your other job? Will you date other women? Sleep with them?"

His laughter rang through the room. "If I stand a chance in hell of being your partner in this life, there is no way in the world I would do that. I wouldn't, I couldn't do that. I don't want to do that."

"I know that men need that, and I would understand if you needed or wanted to do that. Because I'm not so sure I can or will be able to go there."

She watched him stand, moving toward her. When he reached her, he took her hands, pulling her to her feet. Then he picked her up and sat her on the counter, stepping between her legs. He stood there, looking into her eyes. "I'm a full-grown man, capable of making my own decisions and doing what is best for me. Stop worrying about all of this. We are becoming friends. Even if it was offered to me on a silver platter, it's not what I want. I want more than just a one-time thing. This decision I made wasn't because of you." She smirked at him. "I did this for me. It's not what I want anymore. I want to look at my parents and not feel like a schmuck for lying to them. I'm pushing fifty, and I want more. Okay?"

Her hand moved on its own, gently landing on his chest. She could feel his heart pounding in his chest. "Okay."

He squeezed her thighs. "Good. Now, get your shoes, and let's go have some fun." He helped her down, and she went into her room and grabbed her shoes. "Do you know how to ride a bike?" he called out.

"Yes, I don't drive when I'm at home. But I can't ride a bike in a dress," she yelled back.

"Then change. We can rent some bikes on the beach."

She laughed, grabbing her capris.

They spent the morning riding bikes all over the island. They had a seafood lunch at the restaurant at his hotel, then they rode the bikes back to her apartment. "Can I buy you dinner?" he asked her.

She smiled. "I'd like that."

He leaned in and kissed her on the forehead. "I'll be back later. I'm going to go take a shower. I have a few phone calls to return, then I'll pick up dinner and be back."

He watched her eyes when he said he needed to return a few phone calls. She was a bit uncomfortable. He liked that. He wanted to tell her that she had nothing to worry about, but he didn't. He just left.

CHAPTER NINE

On the way to his car, his phone vibrated in his pocket. Pulling it out, he could see that it was Alexander again. This is the fourth time in as many hours. Swiping it on, he answered it.

"Hey, what's up?"

"What the hell? I've been calling you for the last two days."

He laughed. "I'm on vacation. I told you that."

"Well, Kelly James wants a date with you."

"Alexander, I told you I quit. No more dates. I'm out."

"I know, and I told her that, but she wanted me to tell you she'll double your regular rate."

"What does she want?"

"An overnight."

"No way. I'm not interested."

He laughed. "She said if you said no, to tell you she would triple your rate. I don't know what the hell you do to these women, but that's ten grand."

Karl laughed. "I have no desire to do an overnight with her. I'm out. I'm sorry. Ask Tom. He'll do it."

"She wants you."

"I'm not available, and besides, I'm not even in town. I'm on vacation."

"Alone?"

"Yes, alone."

"Well, I can send her to you. Where are you?"

"No, and it's none of your business. Listen, I need to go. I'm about to get in the car. You take care, Alexander."

"You too, buddy, and for what it's worth, I just thought I'd ask. It's ten grand."

Karl laughed. "Yeah, but it's not worth it to me. I'm done."

He disconnected the call and got in the car. He sat there feeling positive that he'd done the right thing. Kelly James was a self-centered snob, and she sucked in bed.

When he got back to the hotel, he showered and then called the gym. Tom answered the phone.

"TKO, this is Tom."

"Hey, it's me."

"Where the fuck are you? Alexander's been looking for you. He told me you up and quit and then took off. Jesus, Karl, what the fuck?"

He laughed. "I'm on vacation for the rest of the week. I'll be back on Sunday. Yes, I quit. It's not what I want anymore."

"What the hell are you talking about?"

"Listen, some shit happened, and I don't want to do that anymore. I think seven years is long enough. It got old, boring. I'm just tired of the nothingness of it. I want a life. I want more."

"Who the fuck are you, and what did you do with my friend?"

Karl laughed. "I'm still me. I'm just not him. Is everything going smoothly?"

"Yeah, everything is fine. I covered all your clients."

"Good. I'm going to have to step back a bit, so get them used to you."

"What does that mean?"

"Well, I think I'm going to do some traveling."

"You're serious about this."

"I am. I need to go. I'll see you on Sunday. Try not to burn the place down."

"Yeah, you take care, buddy."

Karl disconnected the call and got dressed. He ordered food from the Italian place across the bridge and then headed out to pick it up. He grabbed a few bottles of wine and then headed back to Laney's.

When he walked out the door, she wasn't sure how she felt. Was this jealousy? Shaking her head, she decided she wasn't going to let it bother her. She was leaving in a few days to go home, so whatever this was, was just this. A week with an incredibly gorgeous man and no sex. Never again was she going to fall for the sweet nothings a man would whisper. Life didn't work like it did in romance novels. She was sure that every woman on the planet who had ever picked one up and read it, wanted it. But it was unrealistic. This she knew, or believed she knew.

After her shower, she blew her hair dry. If she didn't, it would be wet all night long. Today was her birthday, and she wanted to feel not fifty-five. Laughing to herself, she looked every bit her age. None of it mattered. She had always dressed for herself. As she stood in the closet looking at her summer dresses, she chose one that she hadn't worn yet. It was rather long, and it was just so pretty she didn't want to ruin it by dragging it on the ground. She went full-on, black corset, black panties, and her black thigh high stockings. It was, after all, her birthday, and she wanted to feel sexy, so she was going to. Her dress was a classic wrap-around. She had set the table and then grabbed her tablet and got comfy on the couch. She had edits to finish and send off to her editor. She was about an hour in when someone knocked on the door.

When she opened it, he stood there looking at her. "Wow."

"What?" She sounded shocked.

"Now, that's a dress. You look stunning."

She smiled. "Thank you. What did you bring? It smells fantastic."

He wiggled his eyebrows at her as he walked in. "Italian." She watched him as he walked into the kitchen. He was wearing white jeans and a button-down blue shirt. Shaking her head, she shut the door and followed him into the kitchen. "I grabbed a bottle of white and a bottle of red. Just in case."

They ate, talking and laughing. Laney decided to have a glass of white wine after dinner. They sat outside on the patio to watch the sunset. "So, tell me, Karl, what is it that you do for a living, besides date women for money?"

He laughed. "I used to date women for money. I own a gym with a buddy of mine."

Her giggle came out unexpectedly. "Looking at you, I should have guessed that."

"What, you don't like the way I look?" He faked a hurt face.

"Oh, you look fine. Better than fine, actually. I suppose you wouldn't look like that without working out. I should ask you for some tips on how to firm up this body. After losing all the weight, I could use some tightening exercises."

"How much weight did you lose?"

"One hundred and twenty-six pounds. Took me two years. I told you I had an unhealthy relationship with food."

He sat there looking at her. "Wow, that is some accomplishment."

"I have about thirty more pounds to go to reach the weight I was before Anna went to college." She felt her voice change.

He reached over and took her hand in his, entwining their fingers. She was shocked at how it calmed her. They sat there in silence, watching the sun set over the ocean. The colors in the sky were beautiful. It was one of her favorite places.

Turning her head, she looked at Karl. "This was our place. Mine and Anna's. We came every year for my birthday."

"Well, thank you for letting me share it with you."

Her fingers squeezed his hand, and he turned his head to look at her. Picking their hands up, he smiled at her as he kissed the back of her hand.

Before she knew it, he was getting up to leave. "Get some sleep. I've got a day planned for us if you're game."

"As long as I don't have to go into the water, I'm game for

anything."

"What do you have against the water?"

"Well, the way I see it, sharks don't come in my house; I have no business in theirs."

He busted out laughing, pulling her into a hug. "Fair enough. No water is involved." He kissed her on the forehead. "I'll see you in the morning."

She nodded, and he left.

Sitting on the balcony with her had felt incredible. He had never felt so comfortable with a woman before. They didn't even need to talk. It was just right. Holding her hand was all that he needed at that moment. Karl knew he needed to leave because, if he didn't, he would stay, and it wasn't what they needed. She was finally feeling relaxed with him enough to tell him about Anna.

When he walked out, he saw the confusion in her eyes. Hell, he felt it within himself. But he needed to be this man who was strong for her. As he was waiting for the elevator, it hit him. Turning, he looked at her door. "Son of a bitch. Today is her birthday. That's why she looks the way she does." Before he realized it, he was standing in front of her door. He knocked, not knowing what he was going to say, just knowing he couldn't leave. It took her a few minutes to answer. When she opened the door, his heart nearly broke. Her eyes were red. She'd been crying.

"Did you forget something?" she asked softly.

Reaching up, he slid his hand in her hair, pulling it tight against her head, just like she'd said every woman wanted. Stepping inside, he kicked the door closed, moving her to the wall, his leg landing between hers. Tilting her head up, he slowly moved his head, waiting for her to say no, but she didn't. Brushing his lips across hers, he wrapped them around her top lip and sweetly kissed her lip. His body sparked like an electrical current zapped him. Pulling back, he smiled, and when he heard her gasp, his mouth came down on hers, not hard but firm, and he let it go. Everything he had been feeling went into this kiss, and she kissed him back. Her arms moved around his neck, pulling him closer. He slid his other hand down her side to her thigh. Grabbing her thigh, he lifted her, pressing her into the wall. Their tongues warred, tasted one another's. It was the most sensual kiss he'd ever had. They didn't stop for a long time. He was so hard as they neared the end. He knew she could feel him because he was pressed up against her. Pulling his hand from her hair, he wrapped it around her waist as they parted. "Happy birthday," he whispered on her lips as he went in for more. When he'd had his fill, which he believed in his heart he was never going to get enough, he rested his forehead on hers to catch his breath.

"Put me down, Karl." Her lips were still on his. He slid her down his body, setting her feet on the floor. He waited, thinking for sure she was going to slap him or tell him off. But she did neither of those things. She just stood there, looking at him with a storm brewing in her eyes. His arm stayed wrapped around her, his hand on her neck and shoulder, her body still pressed against his. "Why me?" Her fingers touched his lips.

Closing his eyes as she touched him, he whispered, "I feel you. I've never felt someone like this." He opened his eyes. "You see me."

When she slid her hand around his neck and pushed up on her toes to kiss him, he knew. He knew his life was changed forever now. He couldn't walk away from her if he tried. What he felt when her tongue gently touched his top lip sent chills down his spine. When she pulled back, he didn't want to stop. Her hands gently pushed on his chest, and he moved back. Her eyes not leaving his, she took his hand and stepped backward, into the apartment. Like a happy puppy, he followed her. Neither of them looked where they were going; he just kept taking step after step until she stopped.

"Yes, today is my birthday. I want something I've never had before. Can I have it, Karl?" Her voice purred so sexily.

"Laney, I'm not going to sleep with you." He went to touch her face, and she shook her head with a smile on it.

"Good thing I don't want to sleep with you. But there is something

I want."

"What's that?" He thought he would play her sex kitten game, his heart racing.

She stepped back from him. "I want to touch you. To look at you. I've never seen a man as beautiful as you, as defined as you."

He smiled. Hell, he wanted to grab her and kiss her. "But it's your birthday. Shouldn't you be the one receiving pleasure?" He desperately wanted to touch her.

"This will be my pleasure. So, can I touch you, Karl? You said that no woman has ever taken her time with you, that they just wanted sex from you. I don't want sex, Karl. I want to take my time with you. Can I see you? Look at you? Touch you?"

He was terrified he wouldn't be able to speak. His response was a low growl. "Yes."

She smiled at him. "You mentioned the other day that you wanted to see my stockings, that you wanted to know why I wear a corset."

He nodded. He watched as she slowly moved her hands, as if in slow motion, to her waist. Her fingers pulled at the tie wrapped around her. He watched as her dress slowly opened, exposing a beautifully intricate black lace corset. His heart sped up. She was fucking beautiful. He could see the swell of her breasts.

"I wear it because it makes me feel sexy." Her words were so soft and gentle.

She moved the material away. His eyes moved slowly down her body. She was wearing black panties. Her thighs weren't small, but they weren't huge, and when his gaze landed on the top of her hose, he heard himself moan. Her legs weren't firm and hard, but they were luscious and white against the black lace across the top of her thighs. His gaze slowly traveled back up her body, like a leisurely cruise. When he reached her face, looking into her eyes, he said the only word he could think of. "Beautiful."

Her smile was soft as she closed her dress and retied it. "I want you to promise you won't touch me. This isn't about that. Do you promise?" It was the hardest promise he'd ever made, but he nodded. "Good, now, would you allow me to blindfold you? I've read in books my peers have written that, when you take away sight, the experience is far more intense. Keep in mind, I've never done this before. But it's my birthday. So, would you be willing to try it?"

He couldn't contain his smile. "It's your present, so yes."

Her fingers reached to touch his lips. "Will you kiss me first?" Both of his hands were quick, wrapping around her head, his fingers in her hair. He wanted to be gentle; he needed to be careful with her. The kiss was just as powerful as the one at the door. When she had her fill, she pulled away from him, stepping back to the dresser. He watched her hand move behind her, and then she stepped forward, handing him the sleeping mask. "Will you put this on for me?"

She looked nervous. He took the mask from her. "Laney, this doesn't feel right to me."

"Are you afraid, Karl?"

He watched her eyes dance a bit as she teased him. "No, Laney, I'm not scared." He slipped the mask over his eyes, his heart slamming in his chest. He wasn't scared; he was terrified for her. He couldn't figure out where this was coming from, why she would want to do this. He felt her fingers unbutton his shirt. He put his hand on hers. "Are you sure?"

"I'm sure. I want to do this for you. If you hadn't friended me, then I would still be feeling guilty."

"Why the blindfold?"

"Because I don't want you to see me. I want you to have this experience once in your life, just like you gave me that kiss at the door. I want you to think about nothing except the feeling of my hands on you, not see whose hands they are, but just that they are touching you, feeling you."

He pulled the mask off. "Why wouldn't you want me to see you?"

"Because I'm pretty sure I'm going to enjoy this, and I don't want you to see the desire that is going to be obvious on my face. I don't want to sleep with you. I'm not stupid. I know what we would end up doing, and I don't want to do that. I don't want that regret."

"What makes you think it would be a regret?"

"Because men are never what we make them up to be in our

minds. In my mind, Karl, you are the perfect man—the one we write about, the perfect boyfriend, the perfect lover. But that's not reality. I just want to touch you, to give you something you need. You gave me what I needed last night, and I can't ever say how grateful I am for that. But I can give you this. I want to give you this. After that kiss, I know you want this." Her voice was low. "I felt you on me."

He smiled. "What if what you think is wrong about men?"

He watched her mull over what he'd asked. "So, you don't want to be touched?"

Chuckling, he told her, "Yes, Laney, I want you to touch me. I just want to make sure I'm not crossing a line here. I don't want to ruin what we are building."

"Hence, the mask. You can pretend I'm anyone you want me to be."

He reached for her face, pulling her to his mouth, and he kissed her. "What if I want it to be you touching me? What if it's you I want to touch?"

She pulled her lip between her teeth. "You can't touch me."

"But what if you're who I want to touch? More than once? Like for the foreseeable future?"

"Put the mask on, Karl."

He didn't want to do this, not like this. He didn't want this experience to be cheap. He didn't want her to make him feel like this, like he felt with those women. "Laney, I can't do this. I can't let you do this and not let me touch you back. I want the same from you. I want to touch you. I want to taste every part of you. I want more with you." His words were soft, kind. He watched her eyes fill with unshed tears. She blinked more than a few times to stop them. "Hey." He pulled her to his chest. "I want this more than I want my next breath, but I want you in return. God, do I want you in return. We aren't there yet. Can't you feel it? Can't you feel what is happening here?"

She nodded. "I feel it, but it can't be real. It can't be."

"Why can't it be? Tell me why?"

She pulled out of his arms. "Karl, you are like an enigma. You can't be real. You can't be this perfect man."

"Wait a minute. I am so far from perfect it isn't even funny."

"That's where you're wrong. In the world I've lived in, you are. In the world I know, you are something out of the imagination of a romance writer. In my world, men like you don't exist."

He reached for her, gently putting his hands on her arms. "We are in the same world right now, right here. I am real. I am this man, flawed, standing in front of you, wanting to build a relationship with you. Whether it's a friendship or something more, something like you wanted to take place here tonight."

"Why? Why would you want that with me?"

He laughed. "You don't see you like I do. You see yourself like I see myself. Flawed. You don't see the flaws in me, and I don't see the flaws in you. But they are in both our minds, both of our own eyes. Laney, I just can't do this, not unless you are willing to allow the same from me. Are you?"

She looked at him for a long time. "I can't." Her voice sounded strained as if she was in pain.

He pulled her to his chest. "I know, sweetheart, and that's why we can't. But it's all right. If the day ever comes for us, I'll be more than happy to put this mask back on. Until then, I would like to just be who we are now, grow, and if we never get there, I'm fine with that." He leaned her back so he could look in her eyes. "But I'm hoping, one day, we will be because being blindfolded and at your mercy is something I really think I'd enjoy."

She giggled. "Oh, I know you would enjoy it."

"I did, however, want to do something."

She smiled. "What would that be?"

"This." He kissed her. "This, I like. This, I think we can do as often as you like." He kissed her again.

"Will you stay a while with me?"

"Sweetheart try to keep me away. Come on. We need to get out of this room."

She laughed. "Why?"

"Because that bed is a very dangerous temptation." He reached for her hand, pulling her giggling out of the bedroom. "Why were you crying when I left?"

"You want the truth?"

"Always the truth, sweetheart. Always the truth." He sat down on the stool, pulling her between his legs.

"Because I was disappointed in myself for not telling you it was my birthday. I really wanted to kiss you, and I hoped you would, but then you left. I was upset because I didn't kiss you."

"Well, now you have. Do you feel better?"

She stood there looking at him. He couldn't read her eyes. Her fingers slowly moved up to touch his lips. "Karl, how can this be real?" He closed his eyes at the feel of fingertips.

"It's so real, Laney," he whispered. Opening his eyes, he found hers looking back at him.

"Thank you," she said on his lips as she leaned in to kiss him.

He had been with his share of women. He had kissed many of them, but never had he felt a kiss like this with such tenderness, so much desire. His heart swelled as he held her in his arms. When they finally separated, he put his forehead on hers. With his eyes closed, he let out a shuddering breath. "I don't want to freak you out, but I need to say this. I need you to hear it from me, so you know. So you don't doubt yourself in my eyes. Okay?" She nodded at him. "What I saw in that bedroom, you, when you opened your dress to let me see you, I saw you. You are beautiful, sexy, and yes, so very much, I want you. That moment will stay with me forever. I just wanted you to know that. Okay?"

"Thank you. At that moment, I felt all those things. I felt beautiful and sexy. But I think it was because you were the one looking at me."

"I will always be looking at you. I haven't taken my eyes off you since that first morning in the restaurant." Leaning in, he kissed her. "If I go, are you going to be all right?"

"Yes."

"Remember, a day of fun tomorrow."

She smiled. "Why are you trying to make sure I have fun?"

"Who said this was about you?"

"To be honest, I would rather just stay in. I have a transcript to edit. Maybe we could just lounge around."

He pulled her in again. "I would love to lounge around with you. Maybe we could take a nap on the couch."

She giggled. "I could handle that."

"Then I'll bring breakfast."

"How about I make the coffee? Or I could make us breakfast."

"Or I could make us breakfast."

"What? A man who cooks? No way." She put her hand on her chest. "I think I'm having a heart attack."

He busted out laughing. Taking her hand, he got up. "I do all my own laundry, too."

"Stop it. I'm going to die. The lies, they are too much." She was laughing, and he loved the smile on her face.

He pulled her hard to his chest, his hand wrapping around her neck. Seriously, he said, "Laney, I will never lie to you."

She swallowed hard. Then he raised his eyebrows up and down at her, making her smile. "Nor I you. Now go so I can get some sleep."

He kissed her and walked out the door.

Laney leaned against the door with a smile on her face. "Could he be real?"

"Oh, I'm real. Open the door, Laney."

She spun around and opened the door. Grabbing her, he picked her up, and she wrapped her legs around his waist. Before she knew what was happening, the door slammed, and his mouth was on hers. He took her breath away. "I am absolutely real. This is real."

"Okay," she whispered, kissing him.

He set her on her feet, giving her one last kiss. "Goodnight, Laney."

"Goodnight, Karl."

When he walked out, she locked the door and turned out the lights on her way to bed. After changing, she grabbed her tablet off the charger and crawled into bed. She read for five minutes before her eyelids closed.

CHAPTER TEN

When she woke, she stretched with a smile on her face. She knew it was dangerous for her to feel like this. He was growing on her, taking her heart to a place it had never been, a place she knew could and would destroy her. But she promised herself that she was going to live her life for her, no one but her. It took her nearly three years to come back to the world of the living.

After brushing her teeth and throwing on a sundress, she made her way to the kitchen to make some coffee. Picking up her phone, she turned it on. There were twelve missed calls. Smiling, she scrolled through them, just as the phone rang in her hand. Her heart jumped when she saw the name and picture flash on the screen.

"Hey, beautiful."

"Hi, Nana. I tried to call you yesterday, but it kept going to voice-mail. Happy Birthday."

"I know, and I'm sorry. I just spent the day reading. Thank you."

"I really wanted to come with you this year."

"I know, but school is more important. How are finals going?"

There was a knock on the door. She walked over and opened it, waving him in.

"They're good. I think I passed them so far. But I have Chem and Government tomorrow."

"I'm sure you'll do fine. Any more thoughts on which college you're going to?"

"Yeah, I think I'm going to stay closer to home for the first two years, then transfer to a bigger school."

"Well, that sounds like a plan. Get yourself used to things before you jump right in."

She smiled at Karl, who was in the kitchen.

"I know. Listen, I need to get to class. I'm sitting in the parking lot."

"Okay, beautiful. I love you. I'll call you when I get home."

"I love you, too."

Laney disconnected the call and set her phone down. Karl was in the kitchen, cutting up vegetables, so she sat at the breakfast bar and watched. With each chop, the muscles in his arm flexed. He turned and smiled at her. "Everything all right?"

Nodding, she told him, "That was my granddaughter. She called yesterday to wish me a happy birthday, but my phone was turned off. She was going to come with me this trip, but she had finals, and she needed to get her college applications filled out and sent in."

"Did your daughter have children?"

She laughed. "To be honest, I think Anna was a virgin. I'm not sure. But no, she isn't my biological. It's a long story, but I'm her Nana."

"Well, I like the smile she leaves on your face." He moved toward her, kissing her lightly. "Good morning."

"Good morning. Whatcha making?"

He moved back to the counter. "Omelets. I need the protein. You good with that?"

"Yes, just don't put onions in mine. Can't eat them."

"I don't care for onions, so no onions."

He made them breakfast, and then they got comfortable on the couch. Karl sat at one end and Laney at the other. She had given him another of her books to read while she read her manuscript. For hours, they sat like this. Karl had gotten a bit more comfortable and was lying down. The silence was not awkward for Laney. She couldn't believe how comfortable she felt with him there. Her eyes were getting tired, so she put her tablet down and sat there looking at him. He put the book down and reached his hand out for her.

Smiling, she crawled up his body, her hair falling around his face. "What?" she whispered.

His hands came up and pushed through her hair. Pulling her head down, he kissed her. Slowly, she laid her body on his. When she was completely lying on top of him, her body came alive. She had never felt this before, like an electrical current just suddenly started pulsing through her veins.

He pulled her head back. "You look tired."

"I am. My eyes are bugging."

"Scoot down a bit." His voice was raspy. She did, and he laid her head on his chest, wrapping his arms around her. "Sleep."

"I'm not hurting you?"

His laughter bounced her head off his chest. "No, sweetheart, you are not hurting me."

Laney completely relaxed listening to his heart, and soon fell asleep.

As they lay on the couch with her on top of him, thoughts of a life of comfort passed through his mind. He imagined this with her always. There was no way he could deny what he felt. He was pretty sure this budding friendship was quickly evolving into feelings he wasn't familiar with. He did know that when she left, it was going to be difficult for him. He wondered if she would struggle as well. Her body on his was soft, and he was finding he preferred soft. Her breasts were big, bigger than most, and they were pressed against his chest. He needed to curb his thoughts, or she was going to wake up feeling his cock pressed into her. He needed to get a grip. Scaring the crap out of her was not what he wanted to do. Whatever this is, he wanted it. *Friends. We are just friends.* The longer he lay with her in his arms, the harder it became to keep his thoughts in the right place. She started to move, so he casually rolled her toward the back of the couch. She didn't wake up, so he got off the couch and stood there looking at her.

His hands went to his head. If he had hair, he would have pulled it. He couldn't do this to her; he couldn't let his feelings go. Not yet. No, not yet. He found himself standing on the balcony, looking out at the ocean. His American dream. He'd wanted this dream for as long as he could remember. The last date he'd went on made him uncomfortable. The woman had been a repeat date, and she made him feel as if he belonged to her. In a sense, he guessed he did. She'd bought and paid for his services. Was he a prostitute? No, he didn't believe that he was. But if you put it all under a microscope, he was. He was paid for his time, and when the clock ended, he fucked them. Looking at Laney on the couch, he felt disgusted with himself. She deserved someone so much better than him. His fucking ego was what drove him. Maybe she was right about wanting what you can't have. Maybe, because she was so adamant on not, he wanted her more.

Turning back to the ocean, he tried to remember when he started to feel like he didn't enjoy that lifestyle anymore. It had been months, maybe even a year. The guys always talked him down. Why was he doing it? Was he afraid to be alone? Was he afraid that no one would find him interesting because of the way he looked? Laney had said more than once how beautiful he was. But she wasn't playing any kind of game. She seemed like a very independent woman, but then again, she'd cried because she didn't kiss him. *What did that mean?* Was she so starved for human contact, for a human connection, that she settled and let him come to her? No, he didn't believe that.

When he turned back to look at her, she was sitting on the couch, looking at him. He turned and leaned against the railing. Pushing off, he moved into the room and sat on the coffee table in front of her.

"You're leaving?" she said softly.

"Laney, I'm so confused and scared of how I am starting to feel. It's been four days, well, five counting today, and I have no idea what is happening to me, between us."

She nodded. He made sure he watched her eyes. He didn't want her to cry; he wouldn't be able to handle that. She took a deep breath. "I know. It's all been so surreal."

"Yes. I want to say some things to you, and I don't want you to get upset."

"I promise I won't."

"Being here with you is very comfortable. We spent the majority of the morning not speaking, and it was the most comfortable I think I've ever felt in my life. We didn't need to talk. Then you laid down on top of me, and something inside of me changed. The innuendo was so present that it scared the shit out of me. My mother calls the women I date plastic in stature. When I told her about you, she made a comment about me being attracted to a woman of your stature. I know she meant that you weren't plastic. It wasn't a put down; it was her way of waking my ass up. My whole life, I've had a vision of the type of woman I wanted. I suppose all men do, and you're right; we are assholes. But I've talked to hundreds of them over the years, and not one of them holds a candle to you. In the five-minute conversation we had, I knew you had more brains than all of them combined."

"Well, thank you for that. Karl, are you saying that you are leaving because you are now attracted to me in a more than friends way?"

He smiled. "No, sweetheart. I'm telling you I'm leaving because I need to figure out if I can handle just being your friend. Yes, I want you. Who the hell wouldn't? I am hooked in your orbit, and I want so much more with you." His voice got lower. "So much more." They sat there looking at each other. He watched her eyes; they were an incredible color. He could see that she was struggling. He felt as if he was painting her into a corner, and he didn't want her to feel like that. He never wanted her to feel as if she had no choice in the matter. "I just need a bit of time to breathe and get myself under control. I can't seem to keep my hands or my mouth off you, and I don't want to be the asshole that doesn't give you room to breathe, or a choice. The only thing I want is for you to be a part of my life in any way that *you* choose. But I need to get myself in check. So, I am going to go, okay?"

She nodded. "I understand. Thank you."

He shook his head. "Sweetheart, you never have to thank me for anything. The pleasure is and always will be mine." He leaned forward and kissed her on the forehead.

Laney sat there, watching him walk out the door. Everything he said was so noble. *Is he for real?* He wanted her. He said he wanted her. "What the fuck." Looking down at herself, she couldn't help but wonder if he was doing drugs or something. She had tonight and then tomorrow left, and then she would be home.

She didn't like what was happening to her. In such a short time, she was feeling more attached to him, to his words, to the feeling of completeness, and it wasn't something she was willing to do. Her life was her own now. Not that she suffered in her marriage, but she'd suffered great mental anguish, and that's not what she wanted from her life. Getting up, she went in and packed, knowing she was probably making a huge mistake, but she just couldn't handle this feeling of being suspended in emotion. For fifteen years, she'd lived like this, but Anna made it bearable. Anna was the reason she stayed. But she was gone, and now it was her time to have exactly the life she wanted.

With her bags packed, she pulled some paper from her bag and sat at the table. There was no way she was just going to disappear on this man. His words still rolled around in her head, and the feelings that were brewing inside of her were still very prominent. There was no real explanation for what she was going to do, but she needed to do it for both of their sakes. He was conflicted, and she was terrified. It wasn't fair to either of them.

Karl,

I suppose you would think this is the coward's way out. I know I do. I can't let this go on any longer. I didn't invite you here to start anything with you. If I'm honest, it was difficult for me to be here alone with all the memories. You afforded me the opportunity to maybe have some new memories, and you have. I am forever in your debt for making my birthday such a wonderful day.

The kiss was the icing on the cake for me. The gift I wanted to give you, it scared the shit out of me that I wanted to do something so personal with basically a stranger. To me, you are a walking dream, a man who looks like he belongs on the cover of a book, with all the right things to say and the perfect smile. Yes, a dream.

I heard your words, and they didn't upset me, scare me, or make me want to run. I am not running; I am simply leaving, going home where I belong. You are just as conflicted as I am, the difference being you want more, and I can't be the woman who gives it to you.

Life has a way of repeating itself. Our lives have a way of repeating themselves. The same mistakes, tragedies, the same pattern of behavior. I want to be loved, and I want to love, but you, I'm afraid, cannot be that man. Your life will repeat itself, just as mine will, and us being together will only destroy me when you get bored and leave.

I don't want an exciting life for myself. I want to just sit back and write my stories and watch the grass grow. I know it isn't much, but I honestly had everything a woman could possibly want, and it's gone now. So, I want what I want, and that is to just be who I am.

I can't be what I'm sure you believe I can be, or what you might want me to be. I have to stay true to myself and make sure that my pattern of life doesn't repeat itself simply because I won't survive it emotionally if it does.

You are so beautiful, and you woke me up. Thank you for that. Thank you for taking the time to spend these days with me, and thank you for the beautiful words you've said to me. I will hold them close on those lonely days.

I'm sure I will kick myself for not staying, but if I stay, I'm afraid my feelings for you are going to become something more, and I don't want that. I can't.

Thank you, my beautiful friend, and you are my friend. I can't ever repay you for the happiness you gave me over these last few days. You will always be remembered.

Laney

After reading it over, she put it in an envelope and wrote *Karl with a K* on the front. Grabbing her bags, she headed to the car. On the way out, she stopped at the guard's station and asked if they could give the letter to him when he came back.

The guard assured her that it would be taken care of. She pulled away with a smile on her lips, heading over the bridge and to the highway. It was a long way home, and home is where she belonged, not living a dream that would never become a reality. She didn't want a life full of friends and time-consuming activities. She was supposed to finish her edits, but instead, she spent her days with a dream, laughing, and having fun. Oh, she knew there was nothing wrong with that, but it wasn't what she wanted.

Dreams were meant to be crushed, and before she fell for him and was crushed, she left. She always left. That was her pattern.

CHAPTER ELEVEN

Karl knew that leaving her was the biggest mistake he had made in a long time, but he needed to think. He was in a situation he had never been in before. He'd never been excited about seeing a woman, about spending time with one. He had never been excited to share a meal with a woman who actually ate food. His eyes wanted to see only her, but his heart was warring inside his chest. She was such a beautiful woman—mind, heart, body, and soul. Would he fuck her up? Would he fuck her over? Was he this shallow man who cared more about what others thought? He believed that he wasn't.

He was, however, the type of man who believed he wanted exactly what he had. But was he just brainwashed into achieving the goal he'd set for himself when he came to America? He'd lived the perfect example of the American dream. In the reality of his heart, though, his American dream had changed one morning in a restaurant with just the look of a woman across a crowded room—a woman who could see right through his shit.

She had been hurt beyond repair, but was she just a challenge to him? Karl was sure that wasn't the case because he hadn't known a thing about her when he felt the pull toward her. Sitting here looking out at the water, he knew this wasn't the place he wanted to be, but she didn't want this. She wanted to be left alone. Could he leave her alone?

Hours had passed, and he was still unsure of what he should be doing, how he felt, and fighting with the fact that he didn't want to be here because he wanted to be with her. *Is this what rejection feels like?* She accepted his hand in friendship, but friends don't kiss. They don't lay on one another and sleep. They shared things, they laughed, they cried, they watched movies, went shopping, or got drunk.

Did she want more with him? She was upset when he didn't kiss her on her birthday. But then when he did, she was willing to give him what he wanted most. To be touched, to be enjoyed for more than what he could give her. *Why would she do that?* "Only one way to find out." He stood and headed back to her place. He needed to talk to her, to ask her why she was willing to do that for him.

When he arrived at the guard's gate, the guard smiled at him. "Good evening, Mr. Hagger."

"Good evening. I'm here to see Miss Melvin."

"Yes, unfortunately, Miss Melvin has left."

Karl's heart stopped. "Excuse me? When?"

"This afternoon, a little while after you left. She did, however, ask me to make sure that you got this." The man handed Karl an envelope. His hand shook as he took it from him. Looking at the front of the envelope, he saw it said Karl with a K. It brought a slight smile to his face. Looking up at the guard, he smiled.

"Thank you."

"You have a wonderful evening," the guard said.

Karl nodded and pulled away. He didn't know what to do or how to feel. She ran. He knew leaving her wasn't the best thing to do. He waited until he got back to his hotel room to read the letter. With shaking hands, he gently opened the envelope. As he read her words, his heart sank. She went home. Picking up his phone, he called her, but it went right to voice mail. He sent her a text.

~Please, Laney, talk to me. I'm going to head back to Miami. ~

He felt lost, devastated by her words, by her feelings. Did he fuck her up even more? No, he didn't believe that. He packed his bag and headed back home, back to his American dream.

Walking into his apartment, he headed straight to the balcony, straight to the place he felt the calmest. He came here after every date he had. Every time he slept with one of them, he would come here to re-energize himself. Being with those women was draining. He chuckled when he realized he was out there in response to Laney's letter. He didn't need this as a response to her. This was his habit. She was right about the patterns of their lives. They resorted to them; he'd resorted back to the pattern of his life. But he didn't want this life anymore.

Pulling his phone out of his pocket, he hoped to see a message from her, but he knew he wouldn't. He knew he was going to have to wait until New York to see her again, and he wasn't sure he wanted to wait. Yes, his arrogant asshole behavior was taking over. Karl went about taking care of his life, his business, trying to make the time go faster. He knew she had a twelve-hour drive ahead of her. By the time he had finished everything, it was ten at night. He wasn't sure how long she had been driving, but he was sure it was more than eight hours.

Grabbing his phone off the charger, he pulled up her number, pushing the text button.

~ I know you're driving, but I made a mistake when I left. I should have stayed. I should have told you everything I was feeling. Please call me when you make it home. I know I shouldn't say this, but I miss you. ~

When he pushed send, he took his phone and headed to bed.

Laney drove all the way home. Pulling up to her house, she turned off the car and sat in the dark. She didn't allow herself to think about Karl on her drive. But sitting here in the dark, she was second-guessing herself. With a shaky hand, she pulled her phone out of her bag. Turning it on, she hoped there was a message, but then again, she hoped there wasn't. It would be best for them both if the break was clean; it's what she wanted. She wanted to be just another woman for him. Her heart hoped she wasn't. As her phone lit up and loaded, she saw the message icon. Her heart expanded, but then she wondered if he told her off, if his text was saying good riddance. When she read his first message, she was glad that he was going back to his life. Then she clicked on his second message. Her heart lurched when she read his words. Did she miss him? She felt the loss of him, knowing she wouldn't see him again, but it was for the best. He wasn't real. He was just a dream, a manifestation of something she wanted to believe could be true. She didn't call him; it was three in the morning. But she didn't want to be rude, so she sent him a text.

~ *I'm home and safe. There were no mistakes made. You did what you needed to do, as did I. This would never work. We are living two totally different lives, and I think neither of us is willing to give them up. Thank you, Karl, for the wonderful memories and your time. Until we meet again.*~

She hit send and turned off her phone. Leaving her things in her car, she made her way into the house and crashed. Her body was programmed to get up at seven in the morning, and she hated to waste the day. She got up, had her breakfast, and then unloaded her car, dumping everything on her bed. Grabbing her bike, she headed into town to hit the fresh market and to pick up a few things.

She moved right back into her routine of life, doing the best she could to not think about him. Days went by as she finished her edits and sent her book off to the editor. She tended her garden and prepared for New York and then the drive to Maine. Everything was ready, but she wasn't, but after the last event, she was a bit excited to hear what people thought of her new book. She got her costume out of the storage bins since there would be a costume ball this year. When she finished all her preparations, she sat at her computer and began writing. This was her life. She loved her life. She loved everything about who she was, who she had become without her.

Karl woke, grabbing his phone when he heard the ding. Her message was lit up on the screen. "No, sweetheart. No," he whispered to the dark room. His response was to call her, but it went to voice mail. He wanted to text her back, but he couldn't. He had so much to say to her. Pulling his phone to his chest, he closed his eyes, wanting it to be her. He wanted her in his arms. That's where she belonged. He believed that now more than ever.

When morning came, he went to the gym and worked out, and the entire time he had his phone in his pocket, waiting. He waited for days, and nothing. He couldn't stand it anymore; he wanted to see her, and he didn't think surprising her in New York was the wisest choice. So, he did something he had never done before. He hired a private investigator to find her. He wanted to see her, to talk to her. It took him about a week to find her.

"She lives in a small town in Mississippi, under the name of Mel Cross. I've got her address here." The man handed him a piece of paper.

"Thank you."

"Hey, it was very difficult to find this woman. Are you sure she wants to be found?"

"No, I'm not, but I'm willing to take the brunt of her anger if she doesn't want to see me."

"Mr. Hagger, in my research into this woman, she has been through a pretty traumatic experience. She made it nearly impossible to be found."

"I know. Thank you." Karl got up, walked out of the man's office, and headed home to pack. He called Tom on his way home. "Listen, I'm leaving for a while. I'm not sure when or if I'm coming back."

"Karl, man, what the fuck is going on with you? You've been here, but not here, and now you're leaving again."

Karl laughed. "Honestly, Tom, I'm not sure what is going on. I just know that I will regret this if I don't at least try."

"What are you talking about?"

"Not sure, but I'll let you know either way."

"I'll be here."

"Thanks, man."

When he got home, he called the airport. He was going to drive, but it would be a sixteen-hour drive. He couldn't get a flight out until the next day, so he asked about a private plane. He had never done something like this, but he knew he had the money to do it one time, and he didn't want to wait another minute. It was pricey, but he did it anyway. He packed one bag and headed to the airport. It took him some time to find the private hangar, and then he was off. He was more nervous than he had been when she invited him to dinner. He knew he was over-stepping, but she was in his blood. He needed to explain it to her, but she wouldn't answer the phone. Too many days had passed, and he didn't want her to move away from the way she was feeling. He could see it in her eyes. He could feel it in her touch, in her kiss.

The flight didn't take long. When they landed, he rented a car. The airport was a little over an hour from the town she lived in, and it was coming up on six in the evening when he pulled into town. Turning on the GPS in the car, he put in her address. When he pulled up to her house, he sat in the car, looking at it. His hands were trembling when he got out and walked up the driveway. He knocked a few times, but there was no answer. Remembering she said she didn't drive her car at home, he looked around for her bike. After finding it on the side of her house, he saw her in the back yard. She was on her knees, pulling weeds from her garden. He stood there watching her, his heart beating like crazy in his chest. She sat back on her heels, putting the weeds in a bucket on the ground next to her. He moved slowly toward her as she moved forward again. This time, when she sat back, she had a tomato in her hand, and he watched her put it in the basket on the other side of her, which was filled with other vegetables. He moved around and squatted next to her. Slowly, he watched her turn her head to look at him. What he saw in her eyes tore at his heart. She had been crying, silently crying in her garden. "Aww, sweetheart."

"What are you doing here?" she whispered.

"Don't you know?" He reached up and put her hair behind her ear, his fingers trailing down her jaw. "Don't you know?"

She shook her head. "No, you're not real. Men like you are just made up fantasies. Men like you don't want women like me."

His thumb wiped her tears. "Why?"

"Look at you, then look at me."

"I am looking at you. Sweetheart, I'm sorry I left. I shouldn't have. I should have told you what I was feeling, but I freaked out. I won't do that again."

He watched her stand, moving away from him. "You shouldn't have come here. We can't do this. I can't do this."

"Why?" His voice was louder than he wanted.

She stopped walking. He watched her shoulders square as she turned. He loved the fire in her eyes. "You don't own me. No one owns me. I can do what I want."

He smiled. "Laney, please talk to me. Don't run from me."

"I'm not running from you. I'm running from…" She stood there. "I'm running from me. From me!" she screamed at him. "This isn't real. We spent a few days together, and we kissed. That's all it was. That's all it can be."

"Why?" he shouted. He watched her jump when he yelled.

"Because it's not real!" she yelled back.

He was fast, moving toward her, grabbing her face, his mouth crashing down on hers. Kissing her deep, she didn't fight him, instead kissing him back. Pulling back, he put his forehead on hers. "It's real, sweetheart. It's more real than anything I've ever experienced in my whole fucking life. It's so real."

She pushed on his chest, stepping back. He watched as tears fell on her cheeks, and she shook her head. "Patterns, Karl. You have a pattern to your life. I have one to mine. I fall for the wrong men, and I am gutted. You go from woman to woman. I will fall for you; I think I already have. You will take and then leave, moving on to the next, and I will be gutted. I can't do this. I can't let you do this to me. I won't. We had a lovely time, but that's all it was. It's all it can be. You shouldn't have come here."

"I don't believe that, Laney." His voice was calmer as he moved closer to her. "You don't believe that. I know you feel it; I know you feel what is happening."

She shook her head. "No," she whispered.

He smiled at her. "Yes, you do. I can see it in your eyes. I can feel it in your touch. No woman has ever touched me like you do. I made a mistake by leaving. I should have told you what I was feeling." His hand reached up to wipe her tears. "Don't cry, sweetheart. Your tears tell me you feel it, too. We are both terrified, each of us for our own reasons, and there is nothing wrong with that. I'm here, and I'm not going anywhere. If I have to buy a damn house here, I will, but I'm not going to just walk away from what I believe is the..." He stopped talking. "Don't stop this, Laney. Let us learn and grow."

Shaking her head, she cried, "I need to think. I need you to leave. Please, Karl, I... I... I just need some time."

"I'll be at the bed and breakfast. My phone is on. Will you promise me you aren't going to run?"

"This is my home. I'm not running."

He nodded. Leaning in, he kissed her on the forehead. "I don't want to end this. I need you in my life. I want you in my life."

"What if it's not what I want?"

"Then I will walk away and leave you in peace." His voice was sad, and his head was bowed as he walked away.

Laney watched him walk away. He looked so broken, so defeated. He'd come all the way to Mississippi. Why? Why would he do this? She wasn't anything special. She stepped forward. "Karl." He turned to look at her. She just stood there, looking at him. He was so beautiful; at least, she thought he was. She stepped forward, but he didn't move. Taking a few more steps, she stopped. "Why?"

"Why what, sweetheart?"

"Why me? Why do you want this with me?"

He shook his head. "There aren't words that I can find to make any sense of what I feel, what I felt that morning in the restaurant." She nodded. Neither of them moved. "Laney," he whispered. "I just want to try with you. I want more with you."

"I know. I just wish you could tell me why. It doesn't compute in my brain. But I've done nothing but think of you, about the time we spent together. I can't even write. I just think all day long, trying to figure out what you could possibly want with me, and then I tell myself to shut up. You were there with me, you quit your job, and that kiss… I mean, that was some kiss."

He smiled. "Yes, it was."

"Karl, I'm going to make mistakes. I'm programmed to live a certain way, my pattern. I'm afraid, terrified actually, that I'll make a mistake and then…"

"We are both going to make mistakes. We're human. But I'm confident we will work our way through them. I'm too old to play games, so you never have to worry about that."

She stood there looking at him. "Are you hungry?"

He smiled. "I could eat."

"I can make some spaghetti. I have sauce that I can thaw out."

"Spaghetti sounds good."

"Come on." She turned and headed to the back of the house. When she came back, she had her bucket and her basket. She set the bucket on the porch and headed up the stairs.

Karl followed her, remembering to take his shoes off. When they walked into the house, he was shocked. "Wow."

She smiled as she put the basket on the counter. "I built this last year when I finally decided where I wanted to live."

"You built this yourself?" He was shocked.

Laughing, she said, "No. I designed it, though, and the builder did everything I asked him to do."

Karl looked around. The kitchen was just as you walked in the door. A full-sized stove and oven, and the fridge was one of those old ones. Her bedroom was to the right of the doorway. There were a few steps going up, and all of her books were tucked neatly inside the steps. Her bed was huge, with little night-stands on either side. She had a beautiful purple patchwork quilt on it. Looking to his left, he could see a big couch on one wall and a built-in wall unit on the other. Beyond that, he could see what looked like another set of stairs. He looked up, finding what he first thought was a loft, but it wasn't really a loft. Beyond that, he could see the bathroom. "This is incredible."

She smiled. "Come on in. I'll show you around. I mean, it's obvious you can see everything. But it's the things you can't see that will blow your mind." He followed her. "This is the kitchen. I cook once every two weeks and freeze everything. When I get into writing, I always forget to eat, so this way, I don't have to cook. It's already done for me." She turned, moving toward her bedroom. "This is my room. There are compartments along the floor for my clothes and shoes. Here," she pushed on a panel, "is where I keep my deep freeze." The panel opened against the wall. She pulled on a handle, and a sliding tray pulled out. All of her pots and pans were stored there, and behind them was a little deep freeze. She popped the lid to show him.

"Very cool. You designed this?"

"Yep." She pushed the sliding tray back, closing the panel. "This is where I store all my other stuff." She pushed another panel in the middle, and another tray with full plastic containers slid out. He saw a sewing machine. Looking up, he saw her quilt.

"Did you make that?" He nodded to her bed.

"Yeah, I made everything in here."

He looked around. There were curtains on the windows and throw pillows lying around.

"This..." she began, and he watched her pull the stairs back. He hadn't noticed the tracks on the wall. They went all the way to the kitchen counter. "This is where my washer dryer combo is." She popped the panel, and inside was a washer. She pulled it out, and behind it was more storage.

"Amazing."

She put it all back, moving the stairs back into place. "When I want to sew or do something, or even if I feel like eating at the table, it's right here." He watched as she slid a huge table out from a slot under her bed. Two legs dropped down onto the floor. "The chairs are in there." He turned to look where she was pointing. He pulled the small door open to find two chairs folded up.

She put the table back and then moved into the kitchen. "I have a microwave here, and a dishwasher, then just your basic cabinets." She moved into the living room space. "I just need a couch, so yeah, this is it. I designed this wall unit to house all of my things. Plus, I wanted a little source of heat." He saw the small electric fireplace on the bottom. She was moving again, pointing to the stairs. "This is my office. You can go up if you want. It's a mess. It's my chaos. I work best in the mess." She followed him up the few steps.

"This is amazing."

When they got down, she slid a panel on the wall. "This is my tiny but workable walk-in closet. You have to duck down, but I didn't want to waste the space. It also has a bunch of storage, so it's good. Then there is the bathroom." She turned on the light. There was a huge clawfoot tub with a shower, a sink, and a toilet.

"I'm amazed."

He followed her back to the couch, where she sat on one end. Karl sat at the other. "I'm sorry I ran."

"To be honest, I'm not. It made me realize that I'm the fool. The way I felt that day while you were lying on me," he chuckled, "was not a gentlemanly way to feel."

He watched her blush. "What way was that?"

"Oh, sweetheart, I wanted you in a terrible way. You felt so good. I needed to get myself under control. I want to be a gentleman and respect your boundaries, but that day, I'm sorry for this, but I was so fucking hard I was in pain. You smelled so good and felt even better. But when I came back and you were gone, I didn't expect to feel the way I did."

"How did you feel, Karl?"

Leaning forward, he put his arms on his knees. "I felt scared, gutted, lost. This past week, I've done nothing but yell at people."

"How did you find me?"

"It wasn't easy. I hired a private investigator. I know that sounds extreme, but when you wouldn't answer your phone, I was so worried. It took him forever to find you." He was staring at the floor.

Laney got up and knelt on the floor. Moving his hands, she scooted between his legs. He lifted his head to look at her. Slowly, she reached up to run her fingers along his lips. "I missed kissing you," she said softly as she moved closer. "I'm terrified of the way I feel. It's so much, so fast."

His eyes closed as he enjoyed the feel of her fingers. "I know, Laney."

"Shhh." He felt the heat of her breath on his lips. "Karl." His eyes slowly opened as she pulled her fingers away. "Please don't hurt me." Her lips touched his. "I don't think I would recover." Her hands moved to his forearms. She moved between his hands as she pushed up on her knees. "Can I kiss you?"

His hands touched her sides, his thumbs pressing into the side of her breasts. "Yes," he whispered on her lips.

Laney leaned forward, her hands moving up his arms to wrap around his neck. Jetting her tongue out, she ran it across his lips, and it was over for both of them. Lost in a deep, sensual kiss, she climbed on his lap and straddled him. Their mouths stayed locked as their moans filled the small space.

Karl pulled back, looking at her, with her swollen wet lips and sex laden eyes. He knew what he wanted. His hands moved up to her face, his forearms brushing along the outside of her breasts. When his hands reached her face, he pulled her in for one more kiss. "We need to stop this." His words were kind. She smiled and nodded, but as she moved to climb off his lap, he put his hands on her hips to stop her. She looked at him. "I don't want to stop. I want to take you over to that bed and touch you, kiss you, taste every part of you, and then I want to make love to you."

Her fingers touched his face, his eyes. "I'm not ready for that."

Karl smiled. "Neither am I because I don't think I'm going to be able to stop."

"No?"

Grabbing her tightly, he flipped her onto her back on the couch, making her scream and laugh. He crawled up her body. "No." His mouth covered hers, then he got up, leaving her lying breathless on the couch. He turned and adjusted his cock in his jeans while she laughed. She knew what he was doing, and it made her feel right inside. She pulled herself up and walked past him to get her sauce out of the freezer.

"You should pull your car in the driveway before it gets dark. It's hard to see the snakes in the dark."

He turned and looked at her. "Really?" He looked worried.

Laney couldn't help but giggle. "Really."

"Okay, while I'm out there, I'm going to go and check into the bed and breakfast. Why don't you wait for me, and we can cook together?"

It was her face that caused him some concern. "Listen, not that I am in any way going to tell you what to do or who to do it with, but I think you should be warned."

"I'm listening."

"I stayed there when I came here, so I know Sherry. She owns the place, and she is single. She will eat you alive."

He busted out laughing. "There is only one woman whose mouth I'm interested in."

Laney smiled. "That very well may be, but she places her claim on all the men who stay there. She's obsessive about it. She gets one look at you, and I think you might not be safe at night. And if you turn her down, and she finds out you're here to see me, it will be all over town. I know a few of these people. Granted, I don't talk to a lot of them, but they know who I am. I don't want to be the talk of the town."

He moved to her. "What do you recommend?"

She stood there looking at him, then looked at her bed. "You can stay here with me. You can sleep in my bed."

"Where would you sleep?"

"On the couch or in my office on the blow-up bed."

"I can't let you do that." His voice was a whisper as he leaned in to kiss her.

"Yes, you can."

His mouth covered hers. "I'll consider it." He knew he wanted to stay with her.

Karl went and pulled his car in the driveway. They ate dinner and sat on her porch, talking.

CHAPTER TWELVE

"So, will you stay?" Her eyes watched him.

"Yes, but only because I don't want to get seduced while I sleep."

She laughed, standing. "What if I seduce you?" She went to walk past him.

He reached out, pulling her onto his lap. "You would be the only one who could do it." He kissed her.

"Good to know." She got up and went in to clean up. She hated a dirty kitchen. When he heard her, he went in to help. It only took a few minutes. "Did you bring clothes with you?"

"I did."

"Should you get them?"

"You sure about this?"

"I'm sure. I'll sleep in the loft on the blow-up mattress."

"How about I sleep up there?"

"You're a big boy, and my bed is a king. The air mattress is only a queen, and I think you might weigh too much. I slept on it for months. It's not a problem. Go get your stuff, and I'll get the mattress going."

He watched her pull open the middle compartment. When she was done, she had a bag in her hands that looked like a sleeping bag. "Go," she said to him as she moved past him and headed to the loft.

She could feel him watching her move through the house. "Karl, your clothes." Laughing, he went to the car, and after grabbing his suitcase, he headed back into the house. She was on her bed, moving her clothes out of what looked like a compartment. "You can put your things in here. This place isn't big enough for you to just leave your bag..." She turned to look at him, then at his suitcase. Her smile crept across her face. "You brought a suitcase?"

"I wasn't planning on leaving until I was sure you knew I was serious."

"That's a lot of clothes."

He smirked at her. "I was sure you would need more convincing."

She laughed. "Oh, Karl, there is still a great deal of convincing to be done."

His eyebrows raised. "Hence, the suitcase full of clothes."

She shook her head. "Come on."

He climbed up, sitting on the bed next to her. "Wow, that's a big compartment."

"I think all your things should fit. If not, then there's plenty of room in the closet, which is where your suitcase is going when you're done. I need to go check on the bed." She moved around him, crawled behind him on the bed. She knew he was looking at her, but it didn't matter.

As she moved past him, he couldn't help but look at her. God, her ass was spectacular. He watched her move to the other stairs, then he heard the air pump shut off. He went about unpacking his things. He was finding himself amused at what he was doing and being in the small space. Compared to his apartment, the entire house could fit in his living room with room left over. Chuckling, he said, "You know, this entire house could fit in my living room twice. I think it might be just a bit bigger than the master bath."

"All that space for just you?"

"It's my American dream. But, yeah, all for me."

"Well, I guess it comes in handy when you are entertaining."

His laughter rang through the place. He finished putting his things away and climbed down, suitcase in hand. She led him to the closet and put it in the back with her suitcases. Grabbing sheets and an extra blanket, she stepped out, but he was there, in her way.

Reaching for her, he hooked his hand behind her neck. "I never brought them home. They don't even know my real name."

"It's not my business," she whispered as he moved closer.

"Yes, it is." He kissed her.

The sheets fell to the floor as she wrapped her arms around his neck. Karl couldn't stand it; he picked her up and pressed her against the wall. The kiss took on a life of its own. With his hands holding her thighs, he wanted to press them into her bare flesh. God, he wanted this woman in every way. Pulling back with her bottom lip between his teeth, he gently bit her before letting go.

"Karl." She moaned as her head fell back against the wall.

Chuckling, he let her down. Leaning into her, he pressed his body against hers. "Can I use your shower?" Licking her lips, she nodded. "You going to be all right if I move?"

She looked into his eyes. "I don't think I'm ever going to be all right."

Touching her face, he told her, "Aww, sweetheart, we are going to be fine." He pushed off her, picking up the sheets and handing them to her. He went and grabbed a pair of underwear, his pajama bottoms, and a t-shirt. He hated sleeping in clothes, but this was not the place to get naked.

When he came out of the bathroom, she was still up in the loft, making her bed. He folded his clothes and put them on the floor on top of his compartment. "I have a place in the closet to put your dirty clothes."

He turned to see her looking at him from the loft. "Later," he said as he pulled the covers back. When he got comfortable, he looked up, but she was gone. He could see the light on in her closet, so he grabbed his book and his glasses and started to read. He saw her moving and looked up. The pajamas she had on enhanced her chest. He felt himself getting hard looking at her. She had a flimsy robe on to cover herself, but fuck if she didn't look fantastic. Her hair was in a messy bun on top of her head.

"I'm an early riser. I'll try not to wake you. I ride my bike in the mornings, so I'll be gone for about an hour."

He smiled at her. "I don't have a bike. Maybe we could go later in the afternoon and pick one up."

She tilted her head. "Karl, just how long are you going to stay?"

He crawled to the end of the bed, so he could be closer to her. "As long as it takes. I told you, I'm willing to buy a house. I want this. I need you in my life. Nothing else matters right now."

"You're crazy, you know that?"

He laughed. "Crazy is not a word that women use to describe me."

She laughed, touching his face. "Stud-muffin. Greek God."

That sent him into another laughing fit. "Go to bed, Laney, before I drag you up here and kiss you all night long."

Turning, she laughed. "Idle threats." He watched her turn off the lights as she went.

"Not idle, sweetheart. Truth." He lay on his back, looking up at the loft. He could see just the top of her head as she clicked off the light. He got comfortable and picked up his book. He couldn't concentrate, so he just turned off the light. When he did, the floor around the bed seemed to have a soft light coming out from it. He looked over the side of the bed.

"I'm afraid of the dark." Her voice was soft.

"Not a problem, it's pretty cool."

She was quiet, so he settled in, his arm behind his head.

"Karl?"

"Yeah?"

"Do you call other people sweetheart, other women?"

"No, never. It's what my mother calls me. I've never felt comfortable calling someone I'm on a date with that."

"Why do you call me that?"

"Because you are so much more. Because you mean something to me. Because I..." He stopped. He didn't want to say what was in his heart.

"Because you... what?"

"Because I care." His voice was soft.

"Thank you."

"Never thank me, sweetheart. It was, is, and always will be my pleasure. Now, get to sleep, or you won't get up in the morning."

She giggled. "I don't think I can sleep. There's a man in my bed."

Karl busted out laughing. "Well, there's plenty of room if you want to sleep here."

"With the way you kiss me, I think there might be more than sleep going on."

He laughed. "Oh, sweetheart, we are not ready for that part yet. Not for a while."

"If I was a date, would you?"

"If you were a date, you wouldn't matter to me."

"Hmmm. Goodnight, Karl."

"Goodnight, Laney."

During the night, Laney found herself tossing and turning. She wasn't sure why she felt so uncomfortable. Waking up, she used the bathroom and then got a drink. She stood looking at him in her bed. He was so beautiful. She knew it was wrong, what she was feeling, but God she wanted him. Her fingers touched her lips. He kissed so fucking good. He'd sort of touched her chest. With his hand on her thigh, he'd picked her up like she weighed nothing. When she set the glass down on the counter, she was in some sort of haze, and it hit the counter harder than she wanted. "Sorry," she whispered.

"What's the matter?" He sat up.

"I can't sleep."

"Is it because I'm here?"

She thought she would be brave in the dark. "Yes, and because you are in my bed, and I want to be in there with you, doing naughty things."

He chuckled. "You are more than welcome. The naughty things, well, not sure we are ready for that, but…"

She took a deep breath and moved to the stairs. When she climbed on the bed, she sat next to him. "This is going to sound like I am such a slut, Karl, but my panties have been wet since I got home. I can't shut my brain off. I keep thinking about what could have been, what I should have done. When you kiss me, I swear I lose my mind. Nothing stops the thoughts of what it would be like to sleep with you."

He smiled, his hand landing on her thigh. "Well, climb in, and you'll know in the morning."

She put her hand on his. "You know that's not what I'm talking about."

He pushed up on his elbow. "I know, sweetheart. But I don't ever want you to think that is why I'm here. I want more. I want all of it. That's what I came here to tell you, but I don't want to scare you, freak you out."

"What is more?"

"I want a solid relationship with you. I will take whatever you can give me—a friendship, a relationship—but I'm not having a sensual one with you until we are both sure."

"Why not?" Her voice sounded tiny.

"Because I know how I feel, and if I make love to you and it's only one time, it will kill me."

"Why? It's what all men want."

"Yes, it is, and yes, we take what is offered. But, with you, I'm not taking it just because. I want it all." He pulled her down on the bed. "Come here. Let me hold you. Get some sleep. When it's time for us, we will know it."

"I'm so wanton." She turned her heated, flushed face into his chest.

He laughed. "Sweetheart, I know exactly how you feel." He turned her face to his. "I want you, all of you." His voice was so sexy.

"Thank you."

"Stop thanking me," he whispered on her lips, kissing her. She felt this man. Everything about him was a dream. He was nothing like she thought men were. Well, for now, he wasn't. She couldn't believe she was so willing to give herself to him. He was sex on a fucking stick.

Pulling back, he looked at her. "Where did you go?"

"What do you mean?"

"You weren't in that kiss."

She lay there looking at him in the soft light. How did he know? "I was just thinking that you were a dream, nothing like most men are. I can't believe I am so willing to give myself to you, to have sex with you, to want that with you." She smiled. "You're like sex on a stick, and I'm just finding it hard to believe the words you say to me."

"Well, thank you for the compliments, but my words are the reason we aren't going to make love, or you know, fuck. But, sweetheart, listen to my words and know that I mean this. I will never, and I mean never, just have sex with you. I don't want just sex. Sex is something you have when you don't care about the other person you're with. Sex is for self-gratification, a release. You, sweetheart, will never be for my own self-gratification. You will be my greatest joy."

"See, it's words like those that make women swoon. It's words like those that are in every romance novel on the planet. Swoon-worthy. Millions of women around the world dream of a man who looks like you saying those words to them. We all dream of that, think that is what is supposed to happen when you are getting swept off your feet."

Sitting up, he pulled her to him. "My words to you are real. It's how I feel. If I was in this for sex, you would have been fucked thoroughly, and I wouldn't be here." He watched her swallow. "It's not my intention to have sex with you." He smiled, leaning in to whisper on her lips, "But it is my intention to fuck you thoroughly, to make you scream and then scream again. Okay?"

"Yes."

Leaning in, he kissed her. "Let's go to sleep."

She knew she needed to not be in this bed with him. She knew he was going to wake up with an erection, and she knew she wouldn't be able to stop herself from touching him, so she moved to the end of the bed. "I can't sleep here with you. I want something more right now, and we can't. I can't. I'm not ready for you."

He scooted over to sit behind her, wrapping his arms around her waist. She leaned into him as he kissed her neck. "I know you're not ready for me. I know." He kissed her neck again, sucking her skin into his mouth. "I know because I'm not ready for what you have to give me." His mouth found her ear. "I want all of you, Laney. Not just for tonight or the week, I want it all. I'm in your orbit now. Just don't shut me out."

She turned her head, and he covered her mouth, turning her body, so she was lying in his arms. This kiss felt different to her. It felt as if it was filled with love, something she'd never really felt, not on this level. His hand held her face as he pulled back and looked in her eyes. "Goodnight, Laney."

Licking her lips, she touched his face. "Goodnight, Karl." Slowly, she got up. Her panties were wet, and her heart was slamming in her chest. She knew he was watching her, but she needed to change her panties. When she came out of the bathroom, he was still sitting on the bed watching her. "My panties were wet." She was embarrassed.

"Nothing wrong with that," he said in his sexy voice.

"Goodnight."

"Yes, it has been. Goodnight."

She climbed into the loft and lay down, her mind racing a million miles a minute. Touching her lips, a smile crossed them. *Is he real?* She knew he was. Would he leave her once he'd had what he couldn't have? She wasn't so sure. But men said what they needed to say to get what they wanted. But he hired a private detective to find her. He came to her home with a suitcase. He was there. But she was leaving in four days for New York, then going to Maine. She would be gone for two weeks. Would he come back? Shaking her head, she tried to stop her mind from carrying on. Rolling onto her side, she closed her eyes and finally fell asleep.

～

Karl watched her walk to the bathroom. His nose filled with her scent. He knew he was falling hard for this woman. His cock grew hard. He was glad she wasn't going to sleep with him. His sexual appetite would have gotten the best of him, and that's not what he wanted with her. He wanted to savor her, to touch her in every way. He wanted to love her. Love? Was he falling in love with her? What was love? She was damaged; he knew that. Her feelings about men, he would admit, were true. But not him, not his thoughts concerning her. Hell, he was at her house. He would never have done something like this before, but she wasn't like any woman he had ever known, and he still didn't really know her. His confidence that he wouldn't make a move on her until he knew her better made all this bearable. But God. He reached down to grab his cock, hard for her, so hard it hurt. So hard that he was sure, if he stroked himself, he would come. Looking at the loft, he knew he had to control himself. He was a full-grown man, not some teenager. Chuckling to himself, he felt like a smitten teenager. Rolling over, he closed his eyes. Sleep finally came.

CHAPTER THIRTEEN

When morning came, Laney stretched, looking at the ceiling, her smile automatic. She was no longer embarrassed. She decided she didn't care if he knew his touch, his kisses made her wet. She wanted him. She just needed to get past this obsession she had that all men were jerks. Pulling back the covers, she grabbed her robe and headed down to use the bathroom. Turning her head, she could see him stretched out in her bed, her pillow tucked to his chest. Closing her eyes, she wished it was her there instead of the pillow. When she came out of the bathroom, he was awake. "Good morning." She smiled at him. "Coffee?"

"Good morning. Did you sleep? And, yes, please to the coffee."

She laughed. "Not really. You say all the right things, Karl. Your words, your touch make me very wanton, something I haven't been in a very long time." She was making coffee as she spoke.

"Is that a good thing or a bad thing?"

"Not sure. You going to get up?"

He laughed. "I am, but I have a little bit of a problem, and I don't want to embarrass myself or you."

Laney busted out laughing. "I know I shouldn't laugh. I get the morning thing. I won't be embarrassed, but I can't guarantee that I won't look."

She watched him actually blush. "Now, I'm embarrassed. I don't think I've ever felt like this about a natural thing before."

She slinked over to the stairs. Climbing on the bed, she crawled up to his face. "I felt it on my stomach and my back more than once, Karl. I'm well aware of what it feels like."

He laughed. "Perhaps, but I'm not sure I'm ready for you to visually seduce me."

Giggling, she told him, "Oh, don't be coy. You know, as well as I do, that I've been visually seducing you since we met."

"I feel so dirty." He grabbed her, pulling her down on the bed, covering her mouth with his. She was laughing until he bit her lip. That brought her into the here and now. Her arms wrapped around his neck as she deepened his kiss.

"Never dirty, Karl." She moaned as her leg moved over his and wrapped around his hip. He rolled them over, so he was half on top of her, his erection pressing into her core. "Ahh," she moaned, pressing her heel into his ass. She wanted him to do it again, and he obliged her. "Mmm... Karl," she whispered.

Pulling back, he looked at her with sex laden eyes as he pressed into her again. He watched as her eyes rolled back in her head. "So beautiful," he whispered, kissing her again.

They lay there, teasing one another for a few more minutes as they kissed. "You need some relief, don't you?" Her fingers trailed along his lips.

"I'm fine. I have to be. This," he pressed into her, "is for you, because of you. I'm not going anywhere."

"I'm sorry."

"Don't be. I can feel how wet you are." She blushed. "Don't do that. Don't be embarrassed. I'm wet as well. This is the natural progression of us. It's what is supposed to happen and how it's supposed to happen. When we are ready, these clothes won't be a barrier." He kissed her. "I want all of you."

She lay there looking at him, feeling him pressed into her core. She was so wet; she knew she had at least two orgasms, and he knew it, too. But she wasn't embarrassed. She was so fucking wanton. "Coffee's done. We should get up. I'll close my eyes, so I won't be compelled to look."

His smile warmed her heart. "I just want to say this. When you're ready, you look all you want. Don't think for one minute that I don't look at you, because I do. Trust me, I do." After another kiss, he rolled away from her and off the bed. She watched his back and ass as he walked to the bathroom.

"Wow," she whispered so only she could hear. She got up and poured the coffee, then made them breakfast.

"So, how long will you be gone?" he asked.

She crinkled her eyebrows. "What are you talking about?"

"Your bike ride."

She laughed. "Oh yeah. How long are you staying? You do know I am leaving for New York on Thursday?"

"As long as you let me stay, and yes, I know."

"Well, I thought maybe we could go down to the big city and pick you up a bike. I'm assuming that, once I get back, you'll be coming back here to visit, so it's probably a good idea to get you a bike. I don't drive in town."

"Well, I would love to come back, repeatedly, and I was hoping you would come to Miami."

She got up and walked out the door. Her idea of Miami was not something she wanted. When she heard him walk out behind her, she said, without turning around, "I don't do big cities. This isn't going to work. I'm an idiot to think it could. You have a life there, and my life is here. I'm not leaving here. I'm finally comfortable, at peace here. Or, at least, as close to peace as I'm going to get." She felt his body change. "The idea of us is just that, Karl. An idea. A fantasy. I am not the type of woman to just have sex with random strangers, but it's what I should have done with you. I shouldn't have let this go any further than that. I was going to let you have me in Orlando, the beautiful stranger. But it's not what I want."

"Hey." He touched her, and she pulled away, walking off her porch and into the yard. "So, you've already decided that this isn't what you want. Us?"

Turning, she looked at him. "There is no us. It's that cat and mouse game, wanting what you can't have. To believe that I could be something more is a farce. You live twelve hours away."

"Sixteen," he shouted.

"Whatever. Who can afford to travel like that? You have a business to run, not run up here every weekend? I don't want a weekend love affair. Hell, I don't want a love affair. I don't want the emotional attachment that ultimately ends in nothing."

He was off the porch and grabbed her arms before she had a chance to move. "This isn't nothing. I don't want any kind of affair with you. I fucking want you. I want more, so much more. I've never wanted more with anyone. Nothing I have in Miami means shit to me now. Don't you get it, Laney? Don't you fucking feel this? I'm not imagining this, and neither are you."

She stood there, staring at him. "So what, are you going to give up your life and move to the back-woods of Mississippi?"

"Sweetheart, if I knew I stood a chance in hell of sharing this life with you, for the rest of mine, there wouldn't be a fucking thing in the world that would stop me from selling everything I own to do it."

She swallowed hard. "Really?"

His hands moved to her face, tilting it up. "Really."

"Karl, why would you do that?"

She watched as he closed his eyes. When he opened them, his words were so soft he wasn't sure she heard them. "Because I believe I'm falling in love with you."

He stunned her. She took a step back, her eyes not leaving his. "You don't even know me."

"But I want to. I know how I felt when I pulled up to that guard station, and he handed me your letter. I felt gutted; I felt a loss in here," he put his hand on his chest, "that I have never felt before. I knew then that there was something more, something deeper than I thought. When I went back to Miami and walked into that apartment, I did the one thing I always do when I walk in. I went to the balcony, but that day, I realized it didn't mean anything without you there with me. I want to know you. I want to laugh with you, share with you, and make love to you. These things I know. What I don't know is if you want them with me."

"How is this possible? None of this makes any sense," she mumbled.

"No, it doesn't, and I don't think either of us would feel the way we do if it made sense."

"Look at you. Why would you want to spend your life with me? I'm saggy in all the wrong places. I'm far from fit, and I have no desire to do anything but what I'm doing now. Living in my tiny house, writing my books, tending to my garden. Why would you even consider giving up the life you worked so hard to get to do this?"

"Because that life I worked so hard to get isn't anything compared to what I feel when I'm with you. Laney, none of it means a thing to me. Not now. Not now that I've met you." He paused. "Found you."

Shaking her head, she pulled away from him and walked to the backyard, unable to stop the tears. She had no idea what to think, what to feel. She knew she had feelings for him. Lust. She was so fucking wanton of human touch that her head was spinning. But love? Did she? Was she falling in love with him? He excited her, yes. But love? Could she share her life with him? Her hand reached for her necklace. Closing her eyes, she tilted her face to the sky. *Baby girl, is he for real? Did you send him to me? God, Anna, I wish you were here.* She felt him before he touched her. His arms wrapped around her, pulling her to his chest.

"Laney, I'm terrified. I shouldn't have told you I was falling in love with you."

"Yes, you should have. I don't know what love is. Not really. I know what I feel for Anna, but that's not the same as this."

"Don't shut us down before we get started. Can we move forward? Can we let this grow?"

"I believe we can, yes. I think I might need you in my life more than I want to admit. Karl, I'm so lonely, so wanton of a human connection, that it scares the shit out of me. I don't want this to be a mistake, a dream, a fantasy." She got quiet. "I want it to be real."

He slowly turned her in his arms. "It is real for me."

Her fingers let go of her necklace and moved to his lips. "You are so beautiful."

"Thank you, but I'm a troll compared to you. So, we are going to do this? Have a go?"

"Yes."

His mouth crushed down on hers. "My mom is going to die a thousand deaths when she finds out."

"Why?"

"She is a great fan of yours. She wants me to bring you to her house so you can sign all of her books."

Laney laughed. "Maybe when I get back from my trip, I'll let you take me there. I would love to sign her books."

"About your trip, when we were in Florida, I went ahead and booked a room and tickets for all the events at your book signing. I was going to surprise you. But then you left, and now, here I am. I wanted to go to Maine with you if you'd let me."

"Really?"

He nodded. "I told you, I've been telling you, I'm hooked."

"I am surprised. Come on. Let's go get you a bike."

"My car is bigger, so I'll drive."

By the time they had found a bike to fit his huge body, it was lunchtime. "Let me take you to lunch."

"I'd like that."

They found a nice little Italian place and had a huge lunch, laughing and talking. When they finished, they had been there for over two hours. He felt like a teenager in love on a day date with his girl.

By the time they got back to her house, it was late afternoon. Karl put the bike on the side of the house next to hers, and she went inside.

She was tired, so she crawled up into her bed. When Karl came in and saw her, he locked the door and climbed up, laying behind her to snuggle with her.

Laney rolled over into his arms. "Mmm, this is nice. I'm so tired."

"Yes, it is. Sleep. I got you."

He couldn't believe how easy it was for him to fall asleep in the middle of the day. She was in his arms, where he believed she belonged. This is what he wanted in his life.

An hour or so later, she rolled over. He felt himself come alive when she wiggled her ass against his groin, making herself comfortable. At the contact with her, his cock grew harder and harder. He didn't care anymore. She did this to him. When she finished wiggling, his cock was snuggled in the crack of her fantastic ass, and he couldn't have been happier. He couldn't wait to do this with her naked. His mind wouldn't shut off. He was just getting harder and harder. Her hand came up, taking his and pulling it up to her chest, resting it between her breasts, and she kissed his fingers.

"Sweetheart," he moaned.

"I'm not going to stop this with you. I want this with you. I'm just going to do what feels right, what feels natural. I can feel you, Karl, and I want this with you." She slowly turned, leaving his hand at the base of her neck. He didn't want to be an asshole, but his eyes looked at her breasts. The swell of her chest was very visible. Licking his lips, his eyes feasted on her. Sitting up, she pulled her shirt off and lay back down in his arms. His hand moved to rest on her hip.

"Do you want to touch me?"

"With all that I am, yes."

"I want to touch you. You said I couldn't until I was ready to give you the same. Touch me, Karl, because I am going to touch you when you are done." Her hand moved behind her, and he watched as her bra loosened. She slowly slid her strap off her arm, then moved the bra off her breast.

He moaned when her taut nipple appeared. His eyes moved to hers. "I'm not sure I can do this."

Her smile was soft as she moved his hand with hers, covering her breast with his. Then she reached up and touched his lips. "Yes, you can. I want you to. I need you to touch me, to be comfortable touching me."

He felt his fingers press into the soft flesh, and he moaned. She was so soft. Her nipple pressed into his palm. Lifting his hand a little, he palmed her. He watched as she turned to lie on her back. Karl sat up so he could look at her. Her breasts were huge. He was so hard looking at her. His fingers trailed along the outside of each tit, then each nipple. Her back arched, and she moaned as he touched her. Looking at her body, her legs separated a little, he wanted to see her, to taste her. His fingers trailed down her stomach to her jeans.

"Yes, please," she moaned.

He didn't stop, his finger popping the button, working the zipper. He pulled the material apart to expose her red lace panties. Laney pushed up so her ass was off the bed, his signal to pull her jeans down, and he did. As she kicked them off, he felt himself come a little. He was in fucking heaven looking at her. She was a dream. She was his new American Dream. Looking at her, he knew he was going to spend the rest of his life loving this woman. His fingers moved on their own to trace across her core. He couldn't see any hair or feel it, which had him moaning again. Leaning in, he inhaled as he planted a kiss on her lips through her panties. Her arms moved above her head, and she drew her knees up, her back arched. She was desperate for a release, and he knew it wouldn't take much.

"Fuck, you are stunning."

He pulled his shirt off, wanting to feel her against his skin. He moved her legs, laying them on the bed. Placing his knee between them, he slowly moved up her body, stopping to inhale her scent, his tongue jetting out when he reached her stomach, and he trailed it up her body. He lifted his head when he reached her tremendous chest. His mouth rested just above her taut nipple. He wanted to draw it into his mouth, but he didn't. Instead, he gently licked one, then the other, moving up to look at her. He saw something he never imagined seeing in a woman. He saw comfort, and he saw love in her eyes. Slowly, he laid his body on hers, coming in full contact with her. His mouth found hers as his thigh pressed into her core. He heard himself growl a low tender growl when her arms wrapped around him, pulling his entire body onto hers.

This kiss they shared changed him. He sealed his heart to hers, and he knew, at that moment, that he would love her for the rest of his life. He felt her body shift, and they rolled. He wrapped his arm around her, lifting her onto him as he rolled on his back, their mouths not separating. Her hair spilled around his head, his hands slid down her back, and the back of his fingers ran along the sides of her breasts pressed to his chest. Ending his kiss, she pulled her head up, shifting again to sit up. Her hair was so long it covered her whole chest. He looked at her, seeing her nipples just peeking out of her hair. Shaking his head, he smiled when she saw his chest.

Her fingers were touching him, taking in his whole chest that was covered in tattoos. He watched her as she tucked her lip between her teeth, her eyes full of wonder as she outlined each one. "They're beautiful." He felt her brush his nipples. "I want to touch you. All of you."

His eyes closed as she continued down his body. When she shifted, her core landed on his cock, and his reaction was to push up, so he did, and she grinded against the friction created by their contact. "Aww, God," she moaned out. He felt her shudder. Opening his eyes, he watched her come, her fingers pressing into his stomach, her head falling back. His hands wrapped around her as he sat up, and his mouth latched onto her nipple, causing her to cry out and shake. When her body slowed down, her head fell forward onto his lips. His hands wrapped in her hair, pulling it tight against her head, and he laid her down. When he finished, he stood and took off his jeans. He wanted to make love to her, but he knew this wasn't that the time, so he left his boxers on. He was glad they were black. As he knelt back on the bed, her hands moved to touch him, to outline his cock.

"Sweetheart, I'm going to come," he moaned.

Her fingertips slid under the elastic, and she pulled them down and over his cock. It fell out like it had been trapped and suffocating. But when she wrapped her hand around him, his hips jolted forward.

"God, you're huge. So big." Her hands gently squeezed him,

moving so slowly up and down his shaft. His balls tightened; every fucking muscle in his body was tight as he fought his orgasm. She felt so good wrapped around him, and her touch was so gentle. "Karl, kiss me." His eyes opened, and he dropped to his hands, her hand wrapping around his balls. "Come," she whispered on his lips as she kissed him. His balls contracted up into his body, but she squeezed them as her thumb slid across his head, and that was it for him. He had never come so hard in his life. Pulse after pulse, and when she bit his lip, his mind blew. When he was done, she let go of him. Her hands trailed up his stomach, his chest, to his neck, and she pulled him down on top of her, kissing him.

"So beautiful," she moaned, pressing on his chest. When he rolled, she rolled with him, kissing him deeper.

She could feel his hands on her, touching her everywhere he could reach. He grabbed her ass, pulling her to him, pulling her cheeks apart. Then she felt him rip the seams on her panties. His hands, his fingers gently touched her. She felt his fingertip brush along her core, causing her to moan. He rolled them back over, keeping her thigh on his hip. Pulling back, his eyes locked on hers as he touched her. She went over the edge, and he watched her quake from her release. Her hands reached for him, pulling him to her. They both fell asleep holding one another, him with his boxers down to his thighs, and she with her panties shredded between them.

CHAPTER FOURTEEN

Laney opened her eyes, feeling Karl wrapped around her, holding her like he'd been holding the pillow the previous morning. She smiled big. She wanted to touch him, to make him understand what she was feeling, what she couldn't bring herself to say out loud. Saying it would make it real. She moved her fingers along his back, across the back side of his arm. Slowly, he opened his eyes to see her adoring ones looking back at him. She leaned in to kiss him, which got both of them going all over again. She wasn't sure she had ever felt like this, felt this from a man. He was there with her, in this with her, feeling this with her. When they separated, he smiled at her.

"We're a mess."

"I don't care. Karl, I've never done that. I've never orgasmed like that."

"I know, but I'm not done with you yet."

"Mmm, or me with you. You are so beautiful. I didn't realize you had all these tattoos."

"Do they bother you?"

Her giggle bounced his head. "Not at all. They are incredible, and let me just say they look incredible on your chest. You hide this body well, but I want to see it all. I want to touch all of it." Her voice sounded soft and sexy, which made her giggle.

"I'm yours," he said against her lips. "I'm all yours."

They lay there kissing for a few more minutes. She could feel him getting hard against her thigh. She wanted to feel his astoundingly huge cock inside of her. He was bigger than her vibrator, and that thing was huge.

"Can I tell you something?"

"You can tell me anything."

"I think your cock is bigger than my vibrator. I've never touched one as big as yours."

"You have a vibrator? I think I'm jealous."

She giggled. "I told you."

"Yes, I know, but now you have no use for it."

She busted out laughing. "So sure of yourself."

"Oh, I am." He pressed into her thigh, kissing her. "Why don't you take a shower, and I'll make us something to eat. Then I'll shower, and we can continue this contest of who is bigger, me, or your vibrator."

She was giggling as he pushed up, his cock standing up as he went back on his heels. She stopped, giggling when she saw it. "Oh, God, Karl." Licking her lips, she told him, "So much bigger." Her hand reached out to touch him. She got up on her knees to get a good grip on him, taking his nipple into her mouth and grabbing his balls with her other hand.

"Laney," he cried out, his head falling back as she squeezed his balls. Her grip around him tightened. She bit down on his nipple, and he came like a teenager. "Aww, my..." His cum shot out in long, hot streams into her hand and on her stomach and thighs. When he finished, she kissed his chest and climbed off the bed before heading to the bathroom, leaving him sitting there, completely taken aback by her actions.

When she came out of the shower, she moved into the closet to put on a sundress. Karl had made them a beautiful fruit salad and had everything on the counter. When she walked by, he kissed her on the temple, grabbed his things, and headed into the shower.

Laney headed up to her bed to gather her things. She could smell him, his scent in her bed. Looking at it, she smiled. She couldn't wait for him to make love to her, for him to fuck her. She went to sit outside on her deck while she waited for him. A few minutes later, he came out with the bowls, handing her one. Then he went back in and brought out two glasses of cold water. They sat eating, not saying anything. They didn't need to talk. It was the most comfortable silence she had ever been in.

Setting her bowl down, she drank her water. "Thank you, that was refreshing."

"Yes, it was. I didn't think you would want to fill yourself with another heavy meal. Lunch was huge."

She laughed. "It was, and thank you for being so thoughtful."

He took the bowls in the house. When he didn't come out, she went back in. He was lying on the bed reading. She wasn't sure how she felt or what she should do. She felt like an errant child waiting to be scolded. Her heart stopped; did he just use her? Everything she thought about men was happening to her. She felt her anger building as she stared at the wall. She felt just like she did when Don would get off and then just get up and leave.

What she didn't know was that Karl was watching her. She could feel the tears, her thoughts getting the best of her. Instead of standing there, she spun around and stormed out the door.

When she turned, Karl saw the tears and was off the bed and out the door behind her. She made it to the back yard before he had the chance to touch her.

"Hey, sweetheart. What just happened in there?"

Pulling away from his hand, she took a few steps, trying to rein in her anger. Trying to stop the tears she knew were coming. "Nothing," she managed to get out. "Not a fucking thing," came out with a bit more bite to it.

"Hold on a minute. What the hell just happened?"

She spun around. "Exactly what I said. Not a fucking thing." The tears spilled over her lashes, which pissed her off even more.

"This is why I wanted to wait. We aren't ready for this level of intimacy or commitment. You are not convinced that this is where I want to be."

"No, I'm not. What we just did in there should warrant at least some kind of after effect. Not just you getting up and leaving me there. Or not saying a fucking word to me and then leaving me sitting on the porch alone." He stepped toward her, and she backed up, shaking her head. "No! You are not going to swoon me with your words."

"My words and my actions are all I have to give you."

"Your words are the reason I did what I did with you. They swooned me, tricked me into believing there is a chance for something more, when, in reality, it's just about sex. Having what you can't have."

He raised his voice. "Is that what you think?" She nodded. "Jesus, Laney, what took place in there was the single most beautiful moment I've ever spent with a woman. You aren't letting me feel. You aren't hearing or believing what I am saying to you. You can't be that selfish that you can't consider how I am feeling. You blew my mind in that bed. I want nothing more than to taste every fucking part of you, to take my time with you. But I'm terrified I'm going to freak you out. I am falling so hard in love with you. I feel so comfortable with you that I don't feel awkward not talking all the time. Don't run. Don't do this to what we are building. Damn it, woman, just let it happen. I won't hurt you. I can't."

She stood there, wanting to believe him; she wanted him. She was so scared he was going to be just the dream, the fantasy. She nodded. "I'm sorry. I need to stop believing my own thoughts. I just can't believe how lucky I am to have you want me."

He stepped toward her. "I do want you, so very much. Can we just let this grow, let us be us together? I want to make love to you, but we aren't ready yet. I want to taste you, make love to you with my mouth. I want every orgasm. Can I have them? Can I have you?" He wrapped his arm around her, pulling her to his chest, running his hand through her hair.

"Yes," she whispered. He kissed her softly, deeply.

"Come on. I really don't want to get bit by a snake."

Laney busted out laughing. "Come on, you big chicken."

They walked hand in hand back in the house. "I'm going to head up to the loft. I'm sure my editor has emailed me a million times already."

He kissed her on the temple. Grabbing his book, he went to sit on the couch while she did her work. A few minutes later, he heard her talking. "Hey. What are you talking about? He did what? You didn't tell him where I was, did you?" Karl didn't like the sound of that. "Yes, but you know what state I'm in. I don't care what he said. I signed those papers. Then I'm not going to New York. No, I can't. If he shows up there, he will air my business to everyone." There was a pause, and his heart raced in his chest. "I don't think I'm going to change my mind. No, Alice, this is my fucking life. I don't care if it will hurt my sales. You fucking go. You deal with him. I have more than enough money. Oh, so you're going to hold me to my contract? Fine, but when my contract is done, so am I." He heard something slam on the desk. He put his book down when he heard her scream, "Son of a bitch!"

"Anything I can do to help?" He was really concerned. He wasn't sure he had ever heard a woman in such distress or filled with so much anger. Well, a few of his dates would get shitty when he would leave in the middle of the night, but he never wanted to wake up with someone, not like he wanted to wake up next to her.

"No!" she snapped.

Karl made his way up to her office. Sitting on the top step, he said softly, "I'm right here if you need to yell."

She spun around in her chair. "That fucker called my publisher, wanting to make sure I was going to be at the event in New York. He tried to get her to tell him where I was. He said he wanted to talk to me, make things right. She fucking caved and told him I would be there and that the only thing she knew about where I lived was Mississippi."

"I'm taking it that fucker is your husband?"

"Ex! He's my ex. I signed the fucking papers. I walked out over two years ago. I want nothing to do with him."

"Hey, I'll be with you. He is not going to get near you."

She shook her head. "Apparently, I'm still married to him. Is this the wisest choice here?"

He smiled. "I'll tell you the same thing I told him. It wouldn't matter to me if you were still married to him."

She crinkled her eyes as she looked at him. "You talked to him?"

"I did. After I got you into your car, I went to his room to tell him you were gone. He announced you were still married and accused me of sleeping with a married woman. I smiled at him and told him we weren't sleeping together and that we were just friends. I also told him it didn't matter to me, and Laney, it doesn't. I know how you feel about me. I see it in your eyes and feel it in your touch. I'm not worried about him. But I am worried about you."

"I'll be fine. I'm a lot stronger than I was when I left. I just don't want the drama. This is my job. The drama of him showing up will only give the gossip mongers something more to talk about. I mean, walking around with you is going to stir the pot big time, but envy is the kind of gossip I can handle. I can't handle pity, spitefulness, and the drama. I don't even want to go now."

"What did your publisher say?"

"Oh, that it's in my contract. She has been understanding about my leave, but this is the biggest event this year and I need to be there. I mean, she's right. It is, and I do need to be there to promote my new book."

He moved over to her, pulling her off her chair and into his lap. "I'll be right there with you." His fingers traced along her jaw. "I'll defend your honor."

She giggled. "Will you now?"

"Fuck yeah. I'll go all caveman on him."

This sent her into a fit of giggles. "Thank you."

"Can I kiss you now?"

She nodded as his mouth came crashing down on hers. They ended up lying on the floor and kissing for a long time. It wasn't a hot and heavy petting session like earlier. It wasn't time for that, and Karl knew that. He was learning so much from this woman, about who he was, who he wanted to be with her. She was incredible, so strong and smart, she pulled him into her orbit.

When they finally calmed down, he smiled at her. "You better now? Can I go back to my book?"

Smiling at him, her fingers touching his face, she nodded. "Thank you."

"Never thank me, sweetheart. It's what I want." He helped her up and made his way downstairs, shifting his cock in his jeans. Jesus, he had never met a woman who made him so hard so fast. Looking up at the railing, he smiled. He couldn't wait to make love to her.

CHAPTER FIFTEEN

Laney sat at her desk, looking at the blinking of the cursor on the blank screen, her mind whirling. Her ex was going to prove to be a real pain in the ass now that he had seen her. She knew him; she knew he would cry and pull his 'poor me' shit. But he fucking destroyed her mentally and emotionally, so much so that she couldn't allow herself to feel as deeply as she wanted to with Karl. Touching her lips, she smiled. Maybe if she slept with Karl, she would have the courage to fight Don, to take her stand face to face with him. "I think you should make love to me," she said softly.

Karl was sitting on the couch, his book now laying in his lap, and closed his eyes. "Laney, what's going on?"

"Well, I was thinking. If I have that powerful bond with you, then maybe I will be able to face him and tell him with my words, in person, what he did to me, why I left him."

"Sweetheart, I'm not going to make love to you, until I know this is where you really want to be." His voice turned softer. "I'm falling so in love with you."

"Mmm, you say all the right things."

He chuckled. "Did you ever think that they are the right things because you feel them as well?"

"Perhaps."

He laughed. "Do your work."

She sat there, smiling. *Is he for real?* She would see. Her computer dinged. Flipping over to her email, she saw a new one from her publisher.

Mel,

Turn on your phone. We need to talk.

"Arrrrgggg!" she yelled, picking up her phone. She waited for it to load. After dialing Alice, she said, "What the hell do we need to talk about?"

"Listen, I hired security. He isn't going to get close to you. You need to do this. This event in New York is the biggest for promoting, and you know it."

"I do. I swear to God, Alice, if he gets close to me, I will break our contract, and you will never get my new book. I'm not playing this fucking drama game. You, of all people, should know this is the shit these people live on. Look what the press did to me when Anna died. I refuse to play the game."

"I know, and I'm sorry. But I hired security, so you should be fine. Hey, what costume are you wearing?"

"Cinderella. Took me four months to make the dress."

"I'll be Maleficent. I'll see you there."

"Okay."

She hung up. "Looks like I'm going to New York. She hired security."

Karl smiled. "Good. What about Cinderella?"

He heard her giggle. "The after event is a costume party. I'm going as Cinderella. It took me four months to make the dress."

"Well, then I should go as Prince Charming." He laughed.

She had come downstairs and was standing behind him. "I think you'd make a very dashing Prince Charming."

Karl reached up and pulled her onto the couch next to him. "We shall see. You all right?"

She nodded, her fingers touching his lips. "I'm going to get ready for bed." She leaned in and kissed him. "You stay up and read if you want. I'll put my mask on, no big deal. Thinking about him makes my brain hurt, and I think I was pretty dramatic today, so there's that."

He chuckled. "Not dramatic at all. We are learning about each other. I told you, I am not going anywhere, except to the bed and breakfast so you can sleep in your own bed."

She pushed up. "Like hell, you are."

He busted out laughing, pulling her down next to him. "No, sweetheart, I'm not." They lay on the couch, kissing and talking for a little bit, and he could feel her body calming down. When she started to yawn, Karl made her get ready for bed. He turned off the light in the small living area and went to grab his things. When she came out, he kissed her goodnight. "Goodnight, Laney."

With her hand on his chest, she smiled up at him. "Goodnight, Karl, and thank you."

"You never have to thank me. It was and always will be my pleasure. You get some sleep."

He watched her climb the stairs, and then he went to the bathroom to change and brush his teeth. When he came out, she was standing on the step. She reached her hand out and wrapped it around his neck.

"I need a kiss," she whispered. He dropped his clothes on the floor. Pushing his hand into her hair, he pulled it tight against her head, pressing himself into her, and kissed her long and hard. Pulling back, he smiled at her.

"Get some sleep."

She giggled. "Like that's going to happen." She turned and headed to the loft. She wanted to sleep with him, but she knew it wasn't time yet. Taking a nap was one thing, but she knew they would end up doing what they did this afternoon, and she was pretty sure she would convince him to make love to her, and she didn't want that, not yet. Her biggest problem was herself at this point in the picture. Every man she ever knew had let her down. Were her expectations too high? Did she think she was worthy of some royal treatment, or did she just want someone who was careful with her, but rough when need be? She was determined to make herself shut up. This man was here with her, not expecting anything but to let their relationship grow into whatever it was going to be. Hell, they may hate each other by the time they got back from Maine.

Punching her pillow, she rolled onto her side. She struggled to sleep but eventually fell under.

Karl lay in bed, looking up at the loft. He wanted her in bed with him, but he was sure that he wouldn't be able to stop himself if she were. It wasn't time yet, not after her reaction to his non-reaction to what happened between them this afternoon. Thinking about it, he was rock hard. She pulled two orgasms from him. He couldn't ever remember coming so hard before. He closed his eyes, her beautiful body showing up as if he had pulled a picture out of his pocket.

Her breasts were huge and natural, and he loved the way they spread across her chest when she was flat on her back. Her stomach was so soft and plush; he could faintly see stretch marks he was sure were a result of her pregnancy. And she was bare as a baby's bottom along her core. Most women had at least a strip of hair there. Not Laney. It excited him to no end, the fact that she was willing to do this with him, to get to know one another.

Rolling over, his cock hurt; he was so hard. He couldn't help it. She was spectacular, and he felt so honored to be in her bed, to have given her the first orgasms that were not self-inflicted in twenty-five years. Although, the thought of her vibrator was in the back of his mind, and he smiled at the thought that he was bigger. Closing his eyes, he struggled to sleep but eventually did.

When morning came, Laney jumped in the shower, then dressed in a pair of capris and a fancy t-shirt. She was in the kitchen, making coffee and breakfast when she saw him roll over. "Good morning."

Picking his head up, he looked at her. "Good Morning." His head plopped down on the pillow. "What time is it?"

"Just after seven."

"Come here," he moaned.

Smiling, she climbed onto the bed. He pulled her to him, kissing her. "I couldn't sleep last night."

"Me neither. Karl, I'm sorry about the things we did yesterday. I shouldn't have touched you like that, made you come."

"Mmm, that's why I couldn't sleep. I have never come like that in my life."

She giggled. "Me neither. But it's something I think we shouldn't have done, not yet. I don't think I am mentally ready for this. You saw how I reacted."

Karl placed his hand on her face. "Sweetheart, I agree totally with you, but we are learning to trust. You need to trust that I am not playing you, that the pattern I have followed my whole life has changed. You need to trust that your thoughts about men are wrong when it comes to me. I am totally smitten and seriously falling in love with you. If I knew I could keep my hands and body to myself, I would insist that you sleep with me. But when I think about you and this absolutely luscious body of yours, this happens." He took her hand and placed it on his cock. "I've never met or been with a woman who does this to me."

She wrapped her fingers around him, kissing him. "We should get up before we have a repeat of yesterday. You go take a shower, and I'll finish breakfast." Her hand slid up his cock to his stomach as she pressed on him. He rolled onto his back, but she didn't move. Her eyes moved down his body to his cock, and her mouth watered. She hadn't given a blow job in so long, but the thought of him in her mouth made her swallow hard. Instead of getting up, she moved between his legs and sat back on her heels, looking at him. She didn't ask his permission, but she was prepared to share the same with him if he wanted. Sliding her hands up his steel thighs, her fingers moved under the waistband of his pajama bottoms, and along with his boxers, she pulled them down.

"Sweetheart, what are you doing?" he moaned as his cock slapped his stomach.

When she dropped his bottoms on the bed next to her, she moved back between his legs, spreading him wide. Licking her lips, she looked at him, her eyes traveling up his body. "Karl," she whispered.

Pushing up, she grasped his cock in her hand, and before he could stop her, she had her mouth wrapped around his huge purple head. His hand reached for her head, pulling her off of him. He sat up, pulling her up with him, his mouth covering hers. "No, sweetheart. Not yet."

She looked confused. "Don't men enjoy this anymore?" Her demeanor led him to believe she really thought this way.

He smiled. "Oh, yes, we enjoy that a great deal."

She relaxed. "Then I don't understand."

"Not yet. We are not ready for this. I want everything with you, not just a piece here, a piece there. Do you understand? Thank you for wanting to do this, but I can't let you, not yet."

She smiled, touching his lips. "You are like a walking contradiction for a man."

"No, sweetheart, I'm a man falling in love with the most incredible woman, and I'm going to make sure that you know in every way that, when we share this part of our relationship, I am not ever going back to the pattern my life has been. When we make love, you will be the last woman I ever touch, and I will be the last man to ever touch you."

"So sure of yourself. Random fact about me: I'm beginning to believe in this between us."

"I am so very sure of myself. Random fact about me: I don't say shit I don't mean."

Her fingers moved to his mouth to touch his perfect lips. She had never seen lips like his; they were so plump and soft. She watched as his eyes closed, a slow moan escaping him, his breath warm on her fingers. When she pulled her fingers away, he slowly opened his eyes, and she could see his pupils were dilated in the morning light. Her voice was soft. "Go take a shower, Karl, before I take my clothes off and make love to you."

His hand moved up and pushed through her hair, pulling it tight against her head, and he pulled her face to his and kissed her deeply, laying her back on the bed. When he finished, he climbed off the bed, grabbed up his bottoms, and he pulled them on. Turning to look at her, he shook his head. "So beautiful," he whispered as he moved down the stairs and through the house.

Laney lay on the bed, watching him walk away. Her smile was automatic as her fingers touched her lips. *Is he for real?* God, she hoped he was. She managed to get up and make her bed, then moved to the kitchen. She packed them a small snack for after their bike ride.

When he came out, he was dressed, and they ate and then headed out. They rode for about an hour and then stopped at the park for a little morning picnic. Laney couldn't stop the smile on her face. It felt like it had been permanently put there. As they sat enjoying their fruit and water, they talked and laughed. People walked by, smiling at them. A few waved to Laney, but it was when Sherry walked over that Laney felt a rage of jealousy pump through her body.

"Well, hello, Mel. How have you been? I haven't seen you for a while." Her eyes drifted to Karl. "I suppose you found yourself someone to spend time with at the beach. Maybe I should head down there and see what I can come back with."

"Hi, Sherry. I didn't find him at the beach."

Karl was looking at Laney. "No, she didn't find me at all. I'm the one who found her."

"Well, I'm Sherry. I own the bed and breakfast if you ever need a place to stay, or if your friends come to visit and need a place to stay."

"Thank you, Sherry, but I'm quite comfortable at Mel's."

She laughed. "Really, in that tiny little house? I would think that a man your size would need room to spread out."

Laney turned her head to look at Karl, who was looking at her. He winked. "Plenty of room at Mel's. You ready, sweetheart?" With a huge smile on her face, she nodded. When they got up, Karl folded the little blanket she had brought and put it in her basket. "Sherry, it was lovely meeting you, but we need to get on with our ride."

Laney watched him pedal away, then she looked at Sherry, whose eyes were glued to his ass. "Good to see you, Sherry."

Her eyes snapped up, looking at Laney. "He is a dream. No offense, but when you're done with him, send him my way."

Laney busted out laughing. "Oh, Sherry, you go ahead and take your best shot. We are just friends, nothing more, so go for it."

"Really? What is wrong with you?"

"Not a thing, but I need to go, or he'll get lost. Talk soon." She got on her bike and pedaled up to Karl, who had stopped at the corner.

"Wow," he said, looking back.

Laney laughed. "She told me to send you her way when I was done with you."

"No shit? What did you say?"

"Oh, I told her that she should take her best shot at you, that we were just friends." He grabbed her in his arms, kissing her hard while she laughed. "What was that for?"

"She was looking, and she is one scary woman. I feel so dirty, the way she was undressing me."

Laney couldn't stop laughing. "Come on, big boy. Honestly, she's harmless. Horny but harmless." They headed back to her house, laughing and talking all the way. When they got back, they had some lemonade. "I have some things to cook and freeze, and I need to get everything done for tomorrow."

"I need to change my flight. What airport are you leaving from?"

She smiled. "The one in Jackson. It's two hours away."

"Do you mind if I go with you? I didn't think to ask you. I made my mind up in Florida, when I realized you were leaving and I might never ever see you again."

"I don't mind." Her voice was soft.

"Hey." Karl pulled her to him. "Talk to me. Tell me what's going on in that head of yours."

"The press. Karl, when the press gets wind of this, it's going to be all over the gossip columns."

"No one needs to know we are there together, not unless you want them to know. We can do this any way you want, but I think we need to talk. Come and sit with me." He took her hand, leading her to the couch. "When I would date women, I never used my real name. I was known as Jon Anders. I've been to this hotel more than a few times over the last seven years, with dates, whether it was for a function or just, well…" He felt himself getting uncomfortable, having to confess his sins.

She touched his face. "For sex?"

He nodded. "I don't want to cheapen this between us. But, yes, for sex. I don't think we or I will run into anyone there, but it's possible. Not that any of them would read a book. I just want you to know that people there will call me Jon or Mr. Anders. As much as I want us to walk in there as a couple, I'm afraid that you might be automatically referred to as my date, and I don't want that."

She was smiling. "You don't need to worry about it. I didn't know how to tell you that we couldn't walk in together either. The press is going to be all over me, and I don't want to drag you into the drama. I'm supposed to be staying with Alice, but I don't trust her, so I was going to get a different room, one with an adjoining room. Would you stay in that room, or no?"

"I would love to stay in that room. I'm still going to keep my room, though. So, you're okay with this?"

She touched his cheek. "We are who we are out there, but here, we are just Karl and Laney. Oh, and please call me Mel. No one knows my real name, and I'd like to keep it that way."

"Agreed, if you will call me Jon. None of those women know who I am, and there's this one who was pissed I quit. She offered me ten grand for an overnight date, and I turned her down."

"Jesus."

"What?"

Laney giggled. "Are you that good that she would pay ten grand to fuck you?"

She watched him blush. "I know how to make a woman forget who she is for an hour."

She swallowed hard. "Should I be worried?"

"No, sweetheart. This is where I want to be. You are who I want to be with."

"I mean about the sex we aren't having."

He laughed. "No."

"I'm going to call the hotel and finish my stuff."

She got up in a daze. *Ten grand for sex with him? What the fuck is that?* "By her paying so much money, does that make you a prostitute?"

"She wasn't paying for the sex, so, no, I'm not a prostitute," he said from the kitchen.

Karl went about making his phone calls and securing a seat on the same flight as Laney. Then he called the gym as he walked outside. He wasn't sure he wanted her to hear this conversation.

Tom answered after two rings. "Hey, what the fuck? Where the hell are you, and why aren't you answering the goddamn phone?

"I told you I was going on vacation and that I would see you in a few weeks. Jesus, Tom, it's your place, too."

"I know, man, but I never realized how much fucking work there is."

Karl laughed. "No, because you're too busy fucking the clientele."

"So true, and you used to do it as well."

"Yeah, I'm over it. Listen, I've been thinking about getting out. Do you have enough to buy me out?"

"Two times over, but are you fucking serious?"

"Yeah. I met someone, and well, she isn't a fan of Miami."

"You are going to give up your whole fucking life for some random chick?"

"She isn't a random chick. But, no, just moving it somewhere else."

"Man she better be a fucking Rockstar in bed. What about your apartment and your American dream?"

"I wouldn't know if she was or not, but I think my American dream has changed."

Tom laughed. "So, you're telling me that you are giving up your life for a woman you haven't had sex with?"

"No, what I'm telling you is that I think I'm done. I want something more than all that bullshit. Did you know Kelly James offered me ten grand for an overnight?"

"Yeah, I'd run from that chick, too. She has it bad for you. I guess she is on the warpath that her money couldn't buy you."

"Funny thing is I wasn't ever for sale. My life is going in a direction that is new for me, and trust me when I tell you there is no way in the world I am going to risk fucking this up."

"Well, I'm glad you found what you are looking for. I might be jealous."

"The funny thing is, I wasn't even looking for her. I saw her in a restaurant, and it was like she was who I'm supposed to be with."

"Does she know what you used to do?"

"Yeah, when I got the chance to spend some real time with her, I wanted her to know everything."

"What did she say?"

"She didn't say a damn word. She said that the people we are out in the world are not the same people we are when we are together. It's all behind us. She has some baggage, too. But we are getting to know one another, and we are taking it slow. She's it for me, man. She is it for me. She's fucking beautiful, smart like no one I've ever met, and funny, talented. Her eyes are this crazy blue-green color. When she smiles, the whole fucking world lights up."

"Jesus, you've got it bad. I'm happy for you. So, yes, to answer your question. I will and can buy you out if that's what you want to do. What about your apartment? It's a kick-ass place."

"I'm going to hang on to that for a little while. But, hey, when I'm ready, it's yours. Fair market price."

"Not a problem. Hey, you take care. Call me when you get back, and don't worry about this shit here. Go live your life. Be and do what you need to do. Life is too short. Love ya, buddy."

Karl chuckled. "Love you, too, and thanks, Tom."

He walked back up to the porch and sat on the steps. He knew he was doing the right thing; this felt so right to him, being here with her, leaving that life behind. He wondered if they had a gym here if people would even be interested.

Laney came out and sat next to him. He bumped shoulders with her. "Did you get everything done?"

She nodded. "I did. We now have connecting rooms. So, I thought I would have the bellhop take my things to my room, and then I'll go have a cup of tea."

"Speaking of tea, what kind of tea do you drink that turns the water red."

"Green tea with pomegranate."

He nodded. "Good to know."

"You hungry? I have some stew cooking. I'm going to freeze what we don't eat. It should be ready soon."

"Do you own this land?"

"I do, why?"

"I was just wondering."

She bumped him. "Why, you planning on moving here?"

"If you'll have me," he said softly, touching her cheek. "One day, maybe. When we get back from Maine, I'm going to head back to Miami. I'm selling my half of my gym to my partner."

"Why would you do that?"

He laughed. "The day before I found you, I had a woman approach me who basically wanted me to take her into my office and fuck her."

"What?" Her voice sounded a bit higher than normal. "Seriously?"

He chuckled. "Sweetheart, it's always like that."

"What did you do?" She sounded sad.

"What do you think I did?"

"Not sure you want me to answer that."

He leaned in, his lips on hers. "I told her I had a girlfriend, then I left, and I haven't been back there since." He kissed her.

"Oh."

He laughed. "I managed to get on the same flight as you, so we can go to the airport together. I can drop off my rental."

"Well, if you're going back to Miami after Maine, then I'm going to need to take my car as well, so I can get home."

"This is true."

"Come on. Dinner should be ready. We have to be up at four-thirty and out of here by five."

They went in and had dinner, and when they finished, Karl packed up his suitcase, and Laney sealed everything and put it all in the freezer. They both showered and got ready for bed.

Karl met her in the living room, kissing her. "Goodnight, sweetheart."

She placed her hand on his chest. "Goodnight."

Sleep came easy for them both.

CHAPTER SIXTEEN

When her alarm went off, Laney rolled over, slamming her hand down on it. She hated getting up this early. She was second guessing this trip. Something inside of her knew Don would be there. He was going to air their life in public, and Karl would do the right thing and interrupt it, giving the press exactly what it wanted. When she got up, she pulled the plug on her air mattress and headed down to make coffee. Karl was sitting on the steps when she walked into the kitchen.

"Can we talk?" he asked softly. She nodded. "I have a bad feeling about this, about me and you in that hotel. I'm afraid that I'm going to run into women I know there, and I'm afraid you are going to get upset and want to end this."

She smiled, walking over to him. "I'm afraid Don is going to be there and air our personal life to the public, and you will interrupt him. I worked really hard to get where I am, to be unfindable. I just don't think this is the best idea."

"Me neither. So, what should we do? I can just go back to Miami and meet you in Maine, or I don't have to go at all."

She shook her head. Was he for real? "I don't want to go either. I know it's career suicide if I don't go, but I just don't feel it. Want to just go to Maine and be us?"

He pulled her into his embrace, wrapping himself around her. "It's your career. It's what makes you, you."

"That's where you're wrong." Her arms wrapped around his neck. "Anna made me who I am. I've fought hard to be this woman in front of you. I just don't want anything to come in the middle of what is happening between us. I'm terrified that something is going to happen, and then everything I thought about men will be true."

He kissed her neck. "Not this man."

She pulled back, her fingers touching his lips. "But you were that man. For most of your life, you've been him."

"Not anymore."

"Patterns, Karl. Patterns. I think we should just go to Maine. I can tell Alice to sit at my table and just tell everyone that I have the flu. If they want books, she can take the orders, and I can sign them and mail them out."

"You sure?"

"Not really, but I am sure about one thing."

His smile said it all for her. "What's that?"

"That I don't want to risk what is happening between us. You are slowly winning me over, and to be honest, I am coming willingly. I just keep praying you are real and that I'm not getting played."

Leaning in, he kissed her. "I will never play you. This decision is yours. I've made mine; I can't go with you."

"And I don't want to go without you. I think it's important that we keep building this between us."

"Agreed. Will you come and lay with me for a bit? I promise not to ravish you."

She laughed. "Yes, I will, but I can't make that promise."

Laughing, he stood, and they crawled into her bed, both on their sides, facing one another. Her eyes were slowly closing. "Sleep, beautiful. I'm right here." He reached for her hand. Entwining their fingers, he pulled it to his chest and closed his eyes.

As Karl lay with her, he struggled to not pull her into his arms. He was so sure that this was where his life was supposed to be. There wasn't one doubt in his mind. No one knew either of them here. He looked at her beautiful face, completely relaxed, and could see the defining age lines along her eyes and top lip. But it didn't matter to him; she was stunning. He hoped and prayed that they were going to work out. She had some pretty serious issues herself. He stopped himself more than once from touching her. He let his eyes close and went back to sleep.

When Laney woke, her hand was still wrapped in his. He was so beautiful. She looked at his face; his facial hair was nearly all gray, but she could see the blond in it. She'd never been with a blond-haired man before. She wanted this man. She wanted to make love to him. "Karl, make love to me," she whispered. She wanted him. She needed him, and she needed the love he had for her. She wanted this. She wanted a life with him.

His eyes slowly opened. "I can't, beautiful. Not yet," he whispered, touching her face.

"I know. It's not time yet. But I want you. I can feel you. I can feel this between us. I want this, Karl. Can I have you? Can I keep you? Always?"

"Yes, sweetheart. Yes, and yes." He pushed his hand into her hair, grabbing it tight in his hand, and pulled her head to his. "Yes," he said as he kissed her deeply.

Laney felt herself getting wet, and her nipples tightening against her pajamas. Her back arched into him, and her hips bucked, needing pressure and friction. This man made her body react like no one she had ever known.

"I've got you," he moaned as he lifted her thigh onto his hip, giving her the friction she needed as she grinding her core against his hard body. "I've got you."

In nearly no time, Laney was freefalling into oblivion as he kissed her, his hand squeezing her thigh. "Please," she moaned.

As he pulled back to look into her very dilated eyes, Karl lost himself, rolling over with her under him. His cock pressed into her hip. He wanted her in the worst way. He slipped his hand into her bottoms, his fingers gliding across her bare core. Her legs spread for him, and she was soaked, which caused him to moan. "God, sweetheart. So wet." Her back arched as he brushed along her bud, his fingertip pushing a little inside of her. She was so tight; he was going to lose his mind when he took her. When he slid his finger back across her bud, she cried out as her body shook in his arms. Cupping her core and holding her tight, he felt her pulse again and again. He couldn't stop his hips from moving, grinding into her hip, and he let go, yelling out. His mouth crushed down on hers. She pulled him to her, clawing him, and he went, letting her.

When they calmed down, she started to giggle. "Thank you for that. I'm sorry I sounded like some horny slut."

Karl laughed. "Don't ever apologize for what you want. You needed a release. I gave that to you. I told you, I want them all."

She touched his face. "You released as well."

"I did. Watching you, feeling you pulse like that, I just couldn't stop myself. I think, when we finally make love, we are going to be in this bed for a while."

"I should get some more condoms then. Less mess."

"Hey, I'm clean."

"I believe you. I just haven't had unprotected sex since I got pregnant with Anna."

Karl laughed. "I've never had unprotected sex. But I want to with you someday."

"Yeah?" she whispered.

He nodded. "Oh yeah."

They lay in bed, kissing and touching one another for a long time. Laney pulled away, touching his face. "We should get up."

He laughed. "Why?"

"Well, I need to call Alice. It's going to be a war zone, and I apologize now for the words you are going to hear. I just don't want the drama and the bullshit of him."

"Would you tell me about him, about your marriage someday?"

"There is so much to tell. I did what I did for Anna. She loved him so much. He was good to her, good to me; he just didn't respect me enough to make me feel alive. I was miserable for fifteen years, and I made everyone believe I was this happy, in-love woman. I never disrespected him or said one bad word about him. I just died a little bit each day, and I waited. When Anna graduated, I had already started the paperwork to sell the house. I was getting my affairs in order."

"Where were you going?"

"I was going to move to Boston with Anna. She was going to do her residency, and I figured I could at least feed her, take care of her while she finished. Then I was going to find my own place and just enjoy my life. But then she died, and I was numb. I couldn't think. Every time he touched me, I wanted to throw up. It took me months to come back from that. He went on his yearly vacation to see his kids, and I put the house up for sale the day he left. Remarkably, it sold in three days. I did a fifteen-day closing, put all his things in storage, filed divorced papers, and sent him everything at his kids' house, and I disappeared."

"I'm sorry she's gone. I'm sorry that you suffered like that."

"Thank you. Tell me how you became a date for hire."

"Well, when I was in school, I had this girlfriend. God, I thought at the time that I loved her, and that when we finished school, we would eventually get married. You know the happily ever after thought. She was the first girl I slept with. But she had other plans, I suppose, like sleeping her way through the whole school."

"I'm sorry. That had to hurt."

He chuckled. "It devastated me. In Demark, you have to serve in the armed forces, anywhere between four and twelve months. It's not an option. Well, while I was in, I decided to stay a while. I did welfare work mostly, in foreign countries. So much devastation and horrific living conditions. Starving children, and brutalized women. I made the decision to have a vasectomy when I got out. But, while I was in, I had a group of friends. We all talked about moving to America, where the women were free, and anything was possible." She giggled. "When I got here, I worked in construction until I took my citizenship test. Then I met a few guys at the gym, which I now own, and they told me about this place where you get paid for going on dates with women. It was mostly older women at first. I escorted them to functions, made sure they made it home safely, things like that. Then the younger women discovered me. At first, I didn't sleep with any of them. I wasn't a prostitute. But one night, we were playing poker, and my partner, Tom, asked me if I'd slept with my last date, because apparently, he had, and so had a few of the guys. Then my boss told me that, once the date was over, what we did was our business, but the date had to be officially over."

"I suppose your American dream came true then."

He chuckled. "I felt that it had until I met you." He kissed her.

"Such a charmer."

"So, I did it. At first, it was scary, but then I figured out that if I was good at, then I would get more dates, make more money. After a year, I had made enough to bring my parents here. The next year, we bought the gym. The year after that, I bought my apartment. So, yeah, I was living the American dream. The only problem with it was I had no one to share it with, no one to share my bed with, no one to come home to. Year after year, the lonelier I got."

"Did you sleep with the same woman more than once?"

"Yeah. This one who offered me ten grand, she was a repeat. She wanted me every weekend. But my boss knew that about her because she did it with all the guys."

"Who has that kind of money? I mean, I'm sure you're not cheap."

He laughed. "She was a trust fund baby. Isn't that what you call them, the rich girls who don't know what to do with their time?" She nodded. "She is a very beautiful woman but so full of herself. Never did she touch me. She was selfish and bitchy. In the end, I wanted nothing to do with her. She thought, because she paid for me to date her, she owned me."

"Was she who you were with when you met me?"

"No, that was a different brainless client. None of them wanted to talk about anything other than themselves or other people."

"That's so sad. I'm sorry you felt so lonely."

He rolled over, looking at her, touching her face. "Thank you."

"I feel the need to apologize for begging you to touch me. I've just been without for so long, and I am so fucking horny."

He smiled at her. "You don't ever have to say you are sorry for wanting to be touched, for wanting to be with me. Sweetheart, I will give you orgasms anywhere, anytime you want them."

Pulling her lip into her mouth, she smiled. "But I want to feel you inside of me. I want to make love with you, to you. I want that connection with you."

"Yeah? You sure?"

"Oh, I'm so sure."

He smiled. "Soon, sweetheart. Very soon. I just want to break away from my world because, once I have you, there will be no going back for me."

"Yeah?"

"I know I'm just assuming this, but I need to find a place to live here."

"You were serious?"

"I want a life with you. Do you want one with me?"

"Yes, please." She rolled into his arms. "What would you do with all your time? There is nothing to do here."

"Make love to you all day," he whispered as he kissed her. "I was thinking of maybe opening a gym in town."

"You think?"

"It doesn't matter, as long as I can kiss you whenever I want, and we are in the same place."

"Well, we have a few days before Lobsterfest. We can go look in town and see what's there. I'm sure there are more than a few store-fronts that are vacant."

"Sounds like a plan. I, however, am going to take a shower first. I'm a bit of a mess." He kissed her again and got up. When he turned at the bottom of the steps, his breath hitched when he looked at her. She was stunning, lying on the stark white sheets. Smiling, he shook his head and made his way to the bathroom.

CHAPTER SEVENTEEN

Laney got up and grabbed her phone, turning it on. She finished the coffee while it loaded. Picking it up, she saw a few missed calls from an unknown number. Looking at the area code, she knew who it was. "Son of a bitch," she said as she opened the door and walked out onto the deck. She scrolled to Alice's number. When she answered, Laney yelled, "What the hell did you do, Alice?"

"What are you talking about? Why aren't you on a plane?"

"How in the hell did Don get my number?"

"Oh. Why aren't you on a plane, Mel."

"Because I'm not fucking coming. You do the show. You entertain him. I knew it. I just knew you were going to bring him there. Is he there with you now?"

"What do you mean, you're not coming? You have a contract."

"Fuck you, Alice. You take my table; tell the people I have the flu. I don't fucking care what I have. I'm done. I am so fucking done with you, with this bullshit. I can't believe you gave him my fucking phone number. Did you tell him where I live, too?"

"Wait a minute. It's not my fault you destroyed your perfect life, up and leaving a man like him. Selling your house out from underneath him." Karl heard her yelling and got out of the shower. He made his way to the door, wrapped in a towel. "What the fuck? It was my house. I bought it, not him. His fucking name wasn't on any of the paperwork. Is that the cry me a fucking river story he is telling you? Fuck you. I am breaking our contract. Sue me. I don't give a shit. *No one is going to run my life!*" she screamed into the phone. "Do you hear me, Alice?"

"Mel, I'm sorry. I'm so sorry. You just don't tell anyone what the hell is going on."

"You know why? Because it's nobody's business. It's my business, my personal business, and no one is entitled to that knowledge, not even him. Just forget me. I'll find a new publisher, one who isn't going to give my personal information out to fucking people."

"Wait. Mel, come on."

"Fuck you." She disconnected the call. Karl was standing in the doorway, listening to her. He was shocked at what he was hearing. He watched as she made another call. "What the fuck do you want?"

"Laney, why are you doing this?"

She laughed. "You've got some balls. I didn't want to be mean. I just wanted my life back."

"I thought we had a life."

"That's what you get for thinking. Remember that New Year's Eve right after we got married? The one where you left me sitting on the floor in the family room, in tears, because you said you couldn't make love to me, because you felt like you were being pressured to perform? Well, that was the day I was done. If Anna hadn't loved you so much, I would have left then. I stayed only because of Anna. I was moving to Boston with her, but she died. I couldn't stay married to you; I didn't want to stay married to you. I can't stand you. Just sign the fucking papers, Don, and file them. I don't care if you do or don't, but I will never be your wife again. Don't call me again." She disconnected her phone and threw it across the yard, into the street. Karl watched it break into pieces. He stepped out onto the porch and wrapped his arms around her shoulders. She went to move away, but he held her tight.

"No, sweetheart. I'm here, and I'm not letting you push me away," he whispered in her ear.

Laney leaned into him, her head falling back on his shoulder. "She gave him my number and told him where I live."

"It's fine, beautiful. I'm here."

Turning in his arms, she wrapped them around his neck, pulling herself up his wet body. When his hands grabbed her thighs, she let him pick her up, her legs wrapping around his waist. She felt this man. She wanted him. She needed to feel loved.

Karl turned, moving back into the small house. He pushed her against the door, his hands coming up to her face, pushing through her hair as his lips covered hers. This kiss was different, so very different for both of them. This kiss was filled with love, an emotion he wasn't sure he knew until that moment. He wasn't going to stop this time. This time, he knew. "Laney, I love you, sweetheart," he said softly. He knew it; he felt it. She was who he wanted.

"Oh, God, Karl, if that's what I am feeling, then I love you, too."

He grabbed her ass, pulling her off the wall. "I don't have a condom."

"I do. Side table."

He smiled. "We'll discuss that later. Right now, I want to make love to you."

"God, yes, please."

When he laid her on the bed and sat back on his heels, his cock jetted out of the towel. She reached out to touch him. Releasing the towel, his head fell back while she worked him over. She moved on the bed, her lips clamping down on his nipple, and he was gone, coming like he was fifteen. "Ahhhhh, fuck." It was a long, slow moan, his body twitching as he pulsed.

Laney didn't let him go until every last bit of him had been spent. Karl grabbed his towel and slowly removed her hand, cleaning her fingers and wiping up what he could that wasn't all over her pajamas.

When he finished, he kissed her long and hard. His fingers found the edge of her shirt, and he slowly pulled it over her head. Dropping it on the floor, he looked at her.

He smiled when he saw her sitting up, her massive and perfect chest on display for him. His hands cupped them, squeezing the nipples. He looked at her as her mouth opened a bit. She pushed up so she was on her knees, and his mouth found its way to her taut nipples. He heard himself moan when his lips wrapped around one. His tongue sweetly lathed the hard nub. His teeth clamped down a bit, and she shivered in his hands. He laid her down, moving to pull her bottoms off, panties and all. He wasn't stopping this time. It felt so right, being with her this way. Dropping her panties on the floor, his hand moved to cup her. He had never felt a woman bare like this. She was so smooth, not a stubble was felt. "Roll over, beautiful," he said softly as he bent to kiss her stomach. "Roll over and let me touch you." With a small smile and an open mouth, she turned. "My God." Her plump ass wasn't perfect, but it was perfect to him. His hands were on her, his fingers pressing into the soft flesh. Before he realized it, his teeth were sinking into her ass, licking each spot, gently kissing it. When he finished, she had pink bite marks all over. Moving up her body to the center of her back, he moved her arms, pushing them above her head, and he licked, kissed, sucked, and bit every part of her he could reach. Her moans made him harder as he moved along her body. When he reached her ear, he whispered with his raspy voice, "I want to taste you, sweetheart. Roll over. I want all of you." He was up on his hands as she turned in the space. When she opened her eyes, he saw it; he saw what he felt. He saw love in her eyes. Kissing her with this new feeling between them was incredible for him. "I love you," he said against her lips, his breath warm on her mouth.

She touched his face with her fingertips. "I love you." Lifting her head, she kissed him.

He took his sweet time, moving down her body, spending plenty of time taunting her nipples, making her moan. Down he went, coming to her bare core. Gently, he blew on her. He could see how wet she was. She was going to need to be soaked to take him, with how tight she was around his finger. As he looked at her, his cock hardened even more. His fingers spread her open, her release seeping out, and he nearly came right there. His first taste of love, and he was never going back. She was all he wanted. She felt like silk on his tongue, on his lips. He took her over the edge three times before he'd had his fill, and he wasn't even sure he was done. Moving back up her body, he kissed her so she could taste herself on his lips. "This is what you taste like," he moaned. His cock was at her entrance, and he wanted to push deep inside her, but he didn't. He wanted her again and again. "Sweetheart, I need a condom."

"Drawer," she whispered as she pointed to the drawer.

Karl pulled it open. Grabbing a few foil packets and dropping them on the bed, he tore one open. After rolling it on, he looked at her watching him. Leaning down, he kissed her as her legs wrapped around him. Dropping down on his elbows, he kept his eyes on hers. "Look at me, beautiful. I want to watch you." He moaned as he started the slow push. "Oh, God." His voice came out as less than a whisper. She was so tight around him, so wet. The burn was slow as he based himself inside of her. He stopped. "You all right?" He knew he was big, and she was tight. She nodded.

Karl pulled back, and it began. He made love to her. For the first time in his life, he took his time and willed himself not to come. He felt her release more than once on him. Her warmth, her pulse, she was incredible. They kissed and pulled at one another. His hips flicked a bit harder, his rhythm picking up. He pushed up on his hands so he could watch her tits move with each thrust. Harder and harder, he moved. It was when her back arched, and she gripped him with her core that he lost his shit, coming harder than he had in his whole life.

When his last pulse ended, he came down on his elbows, holding her face in his hands. She had tears on the sides of her face, but her eyes crystal clear. "Karl."

"I know, sweetheart. I know."

"I've never felt that. It was so beautiful; you are so beautiful."

He chuckled. "You are so beautiful. So luscious, so…"

She smiled, her fingers touching his lips. "I love you."

His mouth came down on hers. They lay in bed with him on her, still inside of her, making love with their mouths. Karl rolled over, sliding out of her, and pulled her into his arms to hold her. They must have fallen asleep because, when he opened his eyes, he was semi-hard again. Reaching down, he pulled off the condom and grabbed another one, rolling it on. Laney giggled when he sat up. She was lying on her stomach. "I want to see this ass in the air." He moaned as he pulled her up by the hips. "My God, woman, you're going to be the death of me." He slowly pushed inside of her.

"Oh, God," she cried out.

When he hit the end of her, he paused, but only for a minute. Then he took her slow at first, building his momentum, and he fucked her. He could hear her cries, her grunts with each thrust. His hand slapped her ass, and that was it for both of them. She came harder than he did as he let go. His fingers dug into her hips to the point of pain.

Laney collapsed onto the bed, pulling him from her. He looked down and could see her release on the condom. Smiling, he pulled it off and lay down, wrapping her in his embrace, and his mouth found hers.

Laney lay in his arms. His mouth, his hands never stopped. She had never felt this from a man. Hell, she had never felt lovemaking like this, and she certainly had never been so thoroughly fucked as she was. She couldn't help the giggle that escaped her. "Wow. Yes, please, can I have some more?"

He chuckled. "Anytime, anywhere, sweetheart. You are the most divine, incredible woman. I love you, Laney."

Just then, her stomach growled, and they both busted out laughing. "We haven't eaten since last night." She turned her head and saw it was one in the afternoon. "Karl."

With her back to him, his lips found their way to the bare flesh at the base of her spine. "Mmm, yeah, baby." He moved down to sink his teeth into her ass. Slipping his hand between her legs, he lifted her leg onto his shoulder, his fingers finding his prize. After making a meal of her ass and making her come again with his fingers, slowly, he pulled back, waiting for her to roll over, so he could feast on her nipples. When she did, her hands grabbed his face, and she seared his lips with a fierce kiss, pushing him over onto his back. Swinging her leg over his hips, she climbed on top of him.

"What you make me feel is something out of a dream. You are an incredible lover, Karl."

His hand moved to her cheek. "I am your lover. You are the only lover I have ever had."

Giggling, she said, "I find that hard to believe."

"A lover is someone you make love to more than once. You are the only woman in my adult life that I have made love to more than once in one moment."

"Yeah?" She sweetly kissed him.

Wrapping his arms around her, he flipped her over, making her squeal and laugh. "Yeah. Come on. You need to eat because I've just begun with you. By this time tomorrow, you are going to be lucky if you can walk." She was laughing. Karl sat back and gazed at her ample breasts that shook as she giggled. "Tell me why you have condoms."

"I put them on my vibrator." She blushed. "They have little nubs on them, and it's very stimulating."

"Can I ask you something?" She nodded. "When you came home from Florida, did you use it?"

"Yes." Her voice was shy.

"Did you use it because of me?"

"Yes."

"So, tell me about this vibrator that is challenging my manhood."

She giggled. "I bought it years ago. I needed to have an orgasm, one from penetration. It happens to vibrate and stimulates me at the same time."

He leaned in, his fingers trailing down her body between her breasts, over her stomach, to her core. "I don't vibrate," he said on her lips as his finger slipped inside of her. "But I hum." His lips covered hers, leaning her back. "Let me show you how well." He kissed his way down her body, getting comfortable between her legs. Karl closed his eyes. God, she was so sweet. So beautiful. Her hands fisted the sheets as one orgasm after the other ripped through her. Her cries were soft, but her body was his now. She belonged to him. As he finished her off, he reached for a condom. Rolling it on, he made love to her again. There were no words spoken between them as they lay in one another's arms touching each other softly. His heart was full. His love was deep for her.

"I think my vibrator has outlived its usefulness," she whispered as she outlined his nipple.

Laughing, he rolled onto his side. "My manhood is saved and intact."

"Mmm, it certainly is." Her stomach growled.

He chuckled, leaning over to kiss her. Getting up, he picked up all the condoms on the floor and headed to the bathroom. When he came out, she was sitting on the bed with the sheet around her. "You don't need to cover up. You're beautiful."

"Patterns, Karl. Patterns."

He crawled up the bed, pushed her onto her back, and kissed her. "No more patterns, sweetheart. Let's get you fed." As he pulled away, he pulled the sheet down her body, smiling as he kissed her stomach. "You are stunning."

He moved off the bed and into the kitchen without putting clothes on. His smile didn't waver when he looked at her on the bed. He grabbed some eggs and made them omelets. When he carried them back to the bed, she sat up, taking the plate.

"Thank you."

He kissed her hard. "Don't thank me. You're going to need the substance."

She giggled. "Bring it. You are with a woman who hasn't been satisfied in bed in twenty-five years. I'm pretty sure I'm good."

He just laughed as he stuffed his mouth. His mind was racing a mile a minute. He never wanted to be without her, but he knew he needed to go back to Miami, and he didn't want to leave her. He finished his food. Turning, he took her plate, putting it on the floor.

He grabbed a condom off the table and pulled her toward him. "I don't want to leave you."

"Then don't," she smarted.

His mouth bit down on her nipple. His tongue swiped over it. "I want you, Laney."

Her body shook. "Take me, Karl."

He rolled her nipple with his tongue. "Laney, I want to fuck you."

"Ahhh! Why, Karl?"

"I want to hear you scream. I want you to know what it feels like." His mouth covered hers. "You deserve to be loved, beautiful, and I want to be the one to love you."

"Karl?"

"Mmm, yeah, beautiful?" He was enjoying her neck.

"Fuck me."

EPILOGUE

SIX MONTHS LATER

"Come on, sweetheart. We are going to be late," he called out.

"I'm coming. I was washing my hands." Laney came walking out of the bathroom.

"Jesus, woman."

"What?" She looked down at herself. "Is there a stain or something?" She knew his tone.

Smiling, she looked up and saw he was moving toward her. His arm snaked around her waist, pulling her to his chest, his fingers wrapping around her hair. "You are so fucking beautiful," he whispered on her lips as he kissed her.

Giggling, she pulled back. "If you don't stop, we are really going to be late."

"I can't help it. You make me crazy."

Grabbing her hand, he pulled her through the tiny house while she giggled. "I didn't do a thing but walk out of the bathroom."

"Well, you see," he opened the door, "that's all you have to do." Turning, he shut the door and walked her to the car, opening her door for her. She got in, and he made sure her dress was tucked in. Today was the grand opening of his gym in town. They had worked for months, getting it ready. Nearly all the men in town had memberships and were waiting for today.

Karl and Laney hadn't been apart since she left Florida to come home. He knew what he had when he met her. They spent four days in bed making love, then a week in Maine. He talked her into coming to Miami with him, so he could finalize the sale of his gym to Tom, and to clean out his apartment and put his things in storage. Then he took her to meet his parents, where she gladly signed all his mother's books. They had built onto the tiny house, adding a home gym and two offices, one for Karl and a proper one for Laney. They lifted the ceiling in the walk-in closet, giving them more room, then used the space where the stairs were for the hallway to connect the three new rooms.

Don had delivered her divorce papers while they were in Maine, and life had moved forward for them. She finally made her mind shut off with everything she thought about men. He wasn't anything like the men she knew. Maybe it was because he loved her, truly loved her. Looking at him, she just couldn't believe how lucky she was to have him love her. He was so kind, so giving, so caring. She knew deep in her heart that Anna would have loved him.

Karl had an office put in for her at the gym, so she could spend her days there writing if she wanted. They made it to the gym in a few minutes, which made them both laugh. Laney waited in the car for him to open the door. Taking her hand, he helped her out. The crowd was already gathering outside, shaking hands with him, congratulating him.

At nine a.m. on the dot, he gave a little speech. "I just want to say thank you to everyone who helped along the way and for welcoming me into this community." The crowd cheered, and he cut the ribbon.

Laney stood aside and beamed with pride at how successful the opening had been, and how wonderful he was with everyone, even the children. The festivities slowed down around noon, and Laney was getting tired. When she touched his back, he turned.

"Excuse me for a minute," he said to the man he was talking to. Turning to Laney, he kissed her on the temple.

"Can I have the keys? I'm going to go home. I'm a little tired. I didn't get much sleep last night."

Chuckling, he leaned in. "No, I don't suppose you did. Come on. I'll walk you out."

"No, stay and visit. I'm just going to take a little nap. I'll be back in about an hour."

He entwined their fingers, and they turned, heading to the door. When they reached the car, he opened the door for her, handing her the keys. "I'll close up here and get a ride."

"No, Karl, stay. You deserve this. You worked so hard."

"Thank you, but we don't officially open until tomorrow. You go on, and I'll be there in a bit." He kissed her sweetly. She got in the car and headed back to the house. Karl stood and watched her drive away, then went back inside.

When Laney pulled up to the house, she sat in the car looking at it. This was her sanctuary, the place where she'd finally come to peace with what happened to Anna, with the stupid decision she made all those years ago to marry a man that didn't know how to love her.

It was the place he'd come to for her, the place that he made a home. All those months ago, she was sitting in a restaurant at a book event she wasn't ready for, and he found her. Alice was no longer her publisher. The company had assigned her a new publisher; they didn't want to lose her as a client. Karl had accompanied her to every book event since the New York mess. He always stayed out of her lime-light, letting her be Mel Cross. Her latest book was just about ready to be released, and she was closing in on finishing a new one. Looking around, she spied his bike on the side of the house, remembering that first day when they went to the big city to find it. She thought of the little Italian restaurant they found and frequent now.

Her life had changed, and he was the reason. She loved him like she had loved no other. His friends had a problem with her age and the fact that she didn't have a hard body, but they eventually accepted his truth of how he felt and finally wished him well in his endeavors.

Karl didn't seem to mind giving up his life. Although she couldn't imagine it was much of a life, to begin with. Lonely, no one to share his thoughts with. Between them, they never ran out of things to talk about, and the comfortable silences that used to make her crazy were now just a part of their lives. Words weren't always needed to fill the space.

In twenty-five years, she was sure she had never felt this comfortable, this happy. Putting her head back on the headrest, she closed her eyes and remembered Anna and the life they'd shared. It was so beautiful; it was the greatest experience of her life.

She hadn't realized she was crying until Karl opened the door and pulled her into his arms. "I've got you, sweetheart. What happened?"

She shook her head against his chest. "I was just thinking about Anna, how much she would have loved you. I honestly think she put us both in that restaurant at the same time."

He squeezed her tighter. "I often wonder that myself. I shouldn't have been there. Something just told me to stay that night."

She looked up at him. "I'm so glad that you did. God, Karl, I love you."

His hand threaded through her hair, pulling it tight against her head, and he kissed her. "I love you." He scooped her up and carried her into the house. "Come on. You were tired. Let's have a snuggle and just be."

"I thought you were staying at the gym."

He laughed as he sat her down. "You've been gone for two hours."

"What?" She hadn't realized how much time had passed. "Wow."

He unbuttoned her dress, sliding it off her shoulders. "This," his fingers trailed over the swell of her breasts in her corset, "will always be my favorite thing."

"Take it off, Karl," she whispered.

"Mmm," he moaned as he unhooked all the eyehooks. When he freed her, his hands cupped her breasts. "God, you are beautiful."

Smiling, she turned and went up the stairs, crawling across the bed, lying on her stomach.

His clothes fell to the floor as he followed her path. Kissing his way up the back of her thigh, he bit her ass then ran his tongue up her spine. "Laney," he moaned.

Turning, she looked at him. "I love you."

He felt her to the core of his being. He knew the next words out of his mouth were the right words to say. "Will you marry me?"

Smiling, her fingertips touched his lips. "Yes."

OTHER BOOKS BY CIN MEDLEY

Lyssa's Journey

One Hundred Acres

Broken

Six Months

Winter Harbor

Is This Life

Justice

Beautiful Liar

Within the Ashes

Secrets

Lines Crossed